To Donna,

Thank you a million ways.

SECRETS

A Novel

SECRETS ARE A KILLER

KAT TAUBER

authorHOUSE®

Published by AuthorHouse 02/19/2019

Print information available on the last page.

ISBN: 978-1-5462-7776-7 (sc)
ISBN: 978-1-5462-7777-4 (e)

Library of Congress Control Number: 2019900926

Young adult—Fiction. Secrets—Fiction. Killer—Fiction. Gangsters—Fiction. Isolation—Fiction. Suspense—Fiction. Money—Fiction. Dysfunctional family relationships—Fiction. Additions—Fiction. Siblings—Fiction. Magic—Fiction. Love—Fiction. Forgiveness—Fiction. Mystery—Fiction.

AuthorHouse™
1663 Liberty Drive
Bloomington, IN 47403
www.authorhouse.com
Phone: 1 (800) 839-8640

CHAPTER ONE

Paw and Mama had reason to believe our lifestyle was normal . . . only it wasn't.

CHAPTER TWO

"GYPSIES! You better not make any trouble here or you'll be sorry. Keep movin' right out of town," yells an obese, hairy, dirty, over-all clad man standing in the middle of a dusty, small town street, waving a ball cap like he's shooin' away flies.

This verbal assault is totally unnecessary. See, my family—Paw, Mama, little sister, Scarlett O'Hara, and me—Lady—are walking in tandem, daughters leading, parents bringing up the rear, and truly minding our own business. As for being gypsies—we don't look anything like the gypsies in the books where the females wear funny, mismatched, balloon-like costumes, long braided hair, jewelry—lots of bangles and big hoop earrings, and the males—they're all mean looking with crooked teeth and wild, unkept beards. Nope. We're hygienically appropriate in the limited wardrobe we own, and although we may live a peculiar lifestyle, gypsies? I don't think so.

A few passers-by hesitate and look in the loud-mouth's direction, then at us. He turns to the to them and shouts,

"Hang on to your wallets!"

No one is paying attention. He's one stubborn man and continues his rant,

"You deaf?" he hollers, movin' closer to Paw.

Now, Paw is man of few words but anything but deaf; no way. He can be in a sleep coma and be airborne at the snap of a twig; however, there's speculation, Scarlett O'Hara can't hear because she's still not talkin'. Mama, she's a beauty queen and only smiles and waves; then, there's me: who can carry on an extensive conversation when required. Anyway, this moron is challengin' him—not a smart thing to do—because you see, Paw has a temper. Like a land mine, he explodes when we least expect it. So, it's n-e-v-e-r a good idea to provoke him. In all my years, he's never hit his girls. Would come close with flying fists, but then somethin' strange happens, and he'd stop. And, just like that, in a second or less, he goes from maniac to marshmallow. Took me my whole life to understand why, but for right now, durin' this showdown my stomach feels like a kangaroo race; but, outside my demeanor is nonchalant. Paw let's go of Mama's hand, swaggers towards the troublemaker, and shouts back,

"Marilyn, move on. I'll catch up."

The remaining spectators are quiet. Paw gets right up in the guy's face. I drag on Mama's hand, so I can watch and maybe catch some of their chattin'. Paw seems calm with his hands in his pockets. The lips start movin'. Tryin' so hard to eavesdrop and not watchin' where we're headed, my feet miss the curb and the tumble begins. Mama yanks me up before we become a heap in the gutter. The men quit yappin' and start a major stare down. Paw—fed up with the foolishness—sprints to catch up. Like he thinks it's a threat, the man throws his hat in our direction and heckles Paw,

"Quitter! *What*? You afraid to fight in front of your family?"

Paw stops. I know the temper's comin'. Mama and Scarlett O'Hara are movin' straight ahead, but holy crap, anything can happen. The man is air boxin' Paw like he's Mohammed Ali. Paw just shakes his head as if to say, 'dumbass.' It's all pretty funny, but it would be impolite to laugh out loud. If he continues to aggravate Paw this scenario is not gonna end well. But Paw doesn't budge. He hardly looks like he's even breathing. I'm about to close my eyes and cover my ears to ward off the raucous I think is about to happen; however, Paw surprises me when he leaves the scene, rushes back to Mama and continues our stroll.

"Don't ever listen to rubbish. Name calling is a coward's way to fight. Then fightin' isn't such a good idea either," Paw announces.

I make mental notes when he says amazing things 'cause information like this is bound to come in handy someday—for sure.

#

Later, he drops us off in a roadside park attached to a truck stop. See, Paw is a fixer, a career I understand much later in life, and tonight apparently, he's got work to do. When we sleep outdoors, I'm not afraid; Mama is close by, holding onto her locket that no one is allowed to touch, and there's usually other folks nestled in nylon cocoons campin' out. Countin' stars keeps me occupied. Why be afraid? We have each other.

Tonight, Scarlett O'Hara is zonked out on a blanket that smells putrid—like gasoline. Mama is staring down the road, and I'm over stimulated from the day's excitement, so snoozin' is difficult. About the time the eyelids get droopy, Paw returns and roars,

"Time to go."

Mama is the first to get in. She never pays much motherly attention to her kids, so I'm workin; to wake up Scarlett O'Hara, which is impossible. When Paw sees me strugglin', he picks her up and sets us in the back seat.

We're on the main street when sirens and a parade of police cars speed by. Their beanie lights are flashin'. Nothin' has bothered Scarlett O'Hara; however, I'm so hyper—probably won't settle down for days.

Out of the blue like we've been havin' an intellectual conversation, he offers, "It's better to travel at night, no traffic." *If you say so, Paw.*

I guess it's his way of explainin' this spontaneity. We're always on a real flexible schedule when Paw is fixin.' And, this isn't the first time we've disappeared in the night. It's the way we are. It's not easy adapting to impulsivity and change. What choice to we have? Therefore, I discovered young not to question, doubt or challenge Paw. He makes another profound announcement,

"Lady, family is everything. Don't ever forget it. I'm countin' on you to help me take care of them."

Not sure if this means he's gonna train me to be a fixer, so we have extra money, or he's sayin' he trusts I'll do the right thing for Mama and

Scarlett O'Hara. Surely, he'll enlighten me as time goes on. For now, I'm feelin' he's thinkin' I'm trustworthy and dependable.

He turns up the radio, and they sing with Sonny and Cher. I relax and think about the bully. We're not gypsies, but who we are is a story-worth tellin'. Just sayin'.

CHAPTER THREE

I'm contemplating my family. To think that our story started with a beauty pageant.

Story goes Paw's twenty-five and Mama's, nineteen. It's a balmy, sunny, summer day when she's crowned queen of the *Miss New Albany State Fair*. She's a beauty with long, curly, fiery-red hair, flawless bisque skin, and huge green eyes with eyelashes up to her forehead. Hot pink lipstick frames pearl-colored teeth. Her petite figure—with firm bosoms and a tiny waist—makes her look like a mannequin. Her legs are shapely and toned like a prima ballerina. The pageant ensemble is a delicate, sleeveless, full skirted, short-hemmed, lavender frock made of organza with a white patent leather belt and satin shoes. A silver locket on a chain adorns her neckline.

Paw is handsome, full of charisma, with a bodybuilder physique: tall, trim, and strong with humpy muscles that bulge up and down his arms. His hair is brownish-black and wavy, and slicks it back with gel. He has razor-sharp brown eyes and his olive complexion gives him the appearance of a year-round tan. He's a sharp dresser in his navy cotton-knit shirt, with short, tight sleeves huggin' those muscles and opened to mid-chest to show off his frizzy chest hair, and grey creased slacks with a dark belt and mirror-like buckle. He's the most sought-after bachelor in New Albany; therefore, his presence at the fair creates a minor rumble from the ladies who rub up against him, gigglin' and actin' silly with the hopes they'll catch his eye, or so I've been told. He isn't interested. He's obsessed with the Queen.

There she stands, dignified with a bouquet of long-stem yellow roses, her *Miss New Albany State Fair* sash draped over her torso, and the faux diamond crown secured on top of her magnificent hair. She flashes her famous stop-you-in-your-tracks-grin, and waves the queenly wave: wrist, wrist, elbow, elbow. Well, he's gotta have her, so he waits for the well-wishers to scatter.

"Congratulations, Miss . . . ."

"It's Marilyn," she says.

"Marilyn, I'm Pete Fratelli, and I want you to be my wife."

Now most ladies, if confronted by a strange man proposin', might slap his face for being so forward, or scream, or run, but not Mama. She doesn't make a move or utter a sound. Tryin' to make a great first impression, he asks her again, this time with a little more humility,

"Will you please marry me?"

She tilts her head back and twists her torso and says,

"Maybe."

Paw's about to come undone. Apparently, he's never had to work this hard for a woman and he's never been in situation where he's havin' to wait for an answer. Mama knows she's drivin' him crazy. Paw's next move—comes from having some sort of an epiphany (I guess that's an idea that come to your head when you're really not thinking clearly)—and runs over to one of those vending machines with plastic eggs that hold various rings and things. He plugs the machine with money and lucky for him, first try, gets a ring. Rushing back to Mama, he gets down on one knee, takes her left hand in his right, looks in her eyes, and showin' a bit of nervousness 'cause he's hands are sweaty, he proposes,

"Marilyn, you are my one and only. I will love you forever. Please marry me?"

Just like in those romantic movies. And what does she do? She gets all coy and fakes an almost faint and says,

"Yes . . . but."

Now he's about to really lose it, determined, he says, "Anything."

"Promise me you'll never call me any pet nicknames like Sweetheart, or Cutie, or Honey anything. Furthermore, you won't ever call me little woman, the Mrs. or Mrs. Fratelli, either."

This request is only one of Mama's idiosyncrasies, as I learn later, and this pronouncement could have been a deal breaker. But no. Even though macho Paw wasn't inclined to take orders of any kind, especially from a woman, he's so damn happy and excited in that sexy kind of way—so I'm told—he agrees. Mama, she just stands there waitin' for him to, never did find out what she was waitin' for, but Paw, feelin' like he's in control and anxious to get on with gettin' married, puts his hand seductively on the small of her shapely back, and swiftly guides her through the crowd. She doesn't say a word. His touch makes her shiver even though it's about eighty degrees. When they get outside the fairgrounds, he takes her in his arms and gives her the most breathtaking, long, loving kiss—the kind that plays with your tongue—in that moment, she knew he was the one.

Outside the city limits of New Albany, on that balmy, sunny, summer day—adorned in her queen paraphernalia—they get married by a justice of the peace. The dateless wedding snapshot shows a couple with eyes locked on each other. Written on the back is a notation,

> *Today Mr. Pete Fratelli made me his wife*
> *Left my father's house*
> *And ran away with you.*
> *And that was no bad choice*
> *You gave me everything.*

I think she truly believed that and it seems Paw would do anything to give her everything. After all, he would say over and over, "Life is a journey, an adventure, and what else do we want?" Heck, I can tell you plenty.

As newlyweds, they traveled the country in a Chevy convertible. Mama said it was the best car for a tour of the South because the top didn't go up, and from what she determined from television, the weather in most of those states was perfect for their car. For Mama, though, the best part of their adventure was a drive-in theater. Durin' a stop, she'd beg Paw to let them stay long enough to see at least two movies. If there was no money to park close to the screen with a private speaker box, he'd park outside the entrance, so they could snuggle and try to read lips.

Truth be told, Paw and Mama weren't ready for me. She's got dreams. On a big map, Mama highlights each place they pass through and connects them together. She puts marks on the ones for future trips—making one big circle around the ocean. Travelin' around with no home base, no doubt I muddled their plans substantially, but how I got named is so typical of Mama and her strange ways.

#

In a town called Madisonville, Mama spots a drive-in theater. At the time, the only movie on the program is *Lady and the Tramp*. Paw did his fixin' in the last town, so they have money to roll the Chevy through the gates and close to the speakers and screen. This little movie is about two dogs; yes, dogs—one a prissy Cocker Spaniel, named Lady, who lives with a pretty spiffy family, and Tramp, a homeless rascal of a street dog from the other side of the tracks, which I guess means the neighborhood where street dogs live. Lady has it all, and Tramp has nothing. To hear it from Mama, the dogs fall in love. Tramp wants to show Lady adventure, so he rescues her and off they go to see the world. After they're finished, they lived happily ever after in her massive house. It's not flatterin' to be named after a dog, but Mama, with her big fantasies, insists life can be the movies. She deems me Lady the day she gives birth and tells Paw and anyone who'll listen that I'm destined to be prim and live in a spiffy house on whatever street I want.

"Movies are real life. Even cartoons—where animals talk—they tell real stories. Someday, we're going to live just like the movies," she'll say repeatedly.

Like her I don't have another name, and don't use Fratelli. Mama says many famous women only have one name: like Rihanna, Adele, Madonna, Beyoncé—even Marilyn Monroe; her namesake was usually called—Marilyn. One name is all I need to have it all. And, to add to my pending good fortune, I look like Paw. And, I'm feisty.

They probably would have been satisfied with only me because she's just not interested in my upkeep. A second kid would be a huge imposition; however, sometime while watching, *Gone with the Wind*, Mama gets all weepy. Paw's trying to comfort her, does such a good job she gets pregnant. She's not pleased. I'm only a few months old, and now she really doesn't care about me.

"How in the hell do you expect me to breathe with dirty diapers on this baby?" she screeches in between heaves.

She complains the draft messes up her hair and constantly shrieks,

"Damn it, these fumes are killing me!"

I'm bundled up in an itchy wool blanket and cushioned in a big toilet-paper box in the back. Occasionally, I whimper when I'm hungry or wet. Thank goodness Paw notices and tends to me. Poor Mama is sick for days—or weeks—how would I know?

#

The sickness continues until he finally takes her to a hospital. He asks a nurse to help her to a wheelchair and sits me on her lap. He says he'll be right back. When Mama hears this, she jumps up to leave with him and almost drops me on the floor. The medics rush to help, and before she knows it, she's in a cozy hospital bed with pillows, and I'm in a crib next to her. When they ask her if she wants to feed me, she declines.

"That's Paw's job, and he'll be back any minute," is her matter-of-fact reply.

We're there a while because Mama improves, and I get fat. The doctor tells her this pregnancy is going to be difficult, and she needs bed rest. She just smiles.

Mama is so overjoyed to see her husband, she forgets to tell him the doctor's advice. Paw grunts when he lifts me like I'm too heavy for him.

"We're outta here, Marilyn. We have places to be, and it's time we get to it before you have this baby."

We're halfway out the door when the nurse reminds him, he owes money.

"Let me put my family in the car, and I'll come back and pay," he says as he pushes us out and into the car. He never goes back.

#

Mama tries to stay healthy and take better care of me. She gives me a bottle, and when Paw can find it—she eats cheeseburgers and pickles. In spite of the food, her belly doesn't grow. She tries not to complain, holds her side constantly, and her face always looks like a shriveled-up pretzel. He searches for attractive homes. We sleep in tacky motels. And don't make noise—don't want to get evicted. No need for trouble.

One night, Mama asks Paw if we're on our way to the ocean. Now, always, Mama could ask for anything, includin' the moon, and Paw would simply say, "Yes Marilyn." But tonight, he is far from agreeable and well, you remember the temper? Before Mama can throw the covers over her head, he's rearranging the room; the lamp is in pieces, the television is on the floor, and the only chair with no cushions is legless. Halfway through the rage, rubbing the locket, she screams, "PETE!" Her outburst stuns him: His anger subsides, but it's too late. A red blob falls on the sheet, and Mama can't quit vomiting.

He starts blubbering as he gently takes her to the car.

"Sorry for the tantrum, for rearranging the room. Please don't die."

He's in such a hurry he forgets me in the wooden crate. I had no idea. When he realizes I'm missin', he returns, and now he's really frantic and drives like a lunatic through town to the hospital. In the emergency room, he demands the personnel get with it and help Mama. They arrange her on a gurney and start to move her but she hangs onto Paw with a steel grip.

"Don't you go! I don't care if I ever see the ocean. You have to stay here with me," she cries.

The doctors push Paw put of the way—never a good idea—but under the circumstances, he moves and lets them take her. We wait in a cold, sterile room. An hour or so later, the doctor tells Paw it's a girl.

"She's six weeks premature and just four pounds. She didn't cry when she came out, but she shook her fragile fists," the doctor explains. "She's breathing now and will be okay. Your wife is sedated. I'm sorry to tell you, she can't have any more babies. You can go see her, now."

When Mama wakes up, he holds up the baby. She looks just like her.

"I'm naming her Scarlett O'Hara. And, she'll always only be Scarlett

O'Hara. After all, Scarlett O'Hara was courageous, and never cried, and fought hard for her life. This baby will grow to be the same."

For her entire life, whenever Scarlett O'Hara needs anything, she shakes her fists. Later, Mama takes that as a sign her youngest daughter will be a *Miss New Albany State Fair* Queen because she's got the wave.

With two babies and a sickly wife, Paw has important decisions to make. On discharge day, he's ready. The Chevy has a top, and there's a new toilet-paper box in the back for Scarlett O'Hara. Mama pretends we aren't in the car. The doctor tells Paw this behavior is a type of depression, and the mood will pass. Paw tries hard to make everything nice for her. He sets the map on her lap and tells her,

"Pick a place, any place, and that's where we'll go. We'll get a house, a pool, and buy fancy clothes. The girls will go to school, and we'll live just like the movies. We'll have parties, and you can have your own car. Any kind you want."

She doesn't seem to care. When he tries to kiss her, she turns her head, and he gets a mouthful of hair. Things aren't workin' in his favor for sure.

"Drive!" she demands.

Somethin' tells me he better get busy fulfillin' her wishes. Too young to be helpful, I better grow up *fast* because this family needs a lot of support. And, this dilemma is far from the only one we'll experience. Just sayin'.

CHAPTER FOUR

To my amazement, life moves along without too many hassles. Scarlett O'Hara doesn't grow much and is a passive infant. She just sits and watches everything. Makes no attempt to speak or even mimic anyone. Along the side of the road, Paw picks up a hard, plastic milk box and turns it into a booster seat so I can look outside. I get some height to my stodgy body and swagger like Paw. If I try hard, I can pull at the window crank and roll it up and down. My feet almost touch the floor when I sit up straight. Scarlett O'Hara is so small that we can lie toe to toe across the back seat. When Paw has time, he reads aloud the newspapers, racing forms, and bookie sheets. These literary moments become beneficial to my education; by ten years old, I'm a math wizard.

Most days—in between smokes and liquor—Mama rubs her locket and stares—straight ahead—not looking around to take in the scenery, and if she ever looks back at her daughters, she only glares with those emotionless green eyes. Over time, she is moodier and more withdrawn. Her smoking and drinking escalate—especially if he shows more affection and attention to us. When that happens, holy crap!—she goes on a major drinkin' spree. Then we have to deal with the volcanic aftermath and watch her insides become outsides. Poor Paw.

True to eccentricities, no one talks about ages, and since I've been on the road for most of my life to-date, I'm thinkin', I might be twelve. A girl can experience a lot of life, livin' the way we do—so I'm kinda growin' up fast. Anyway, in a town called Bakersfield, the Chevy is low on gas. Paw pulls into a filling station with a convenience store. Damn independent by this time, I jump out to get something to drink. The man behind the counter is busy with his money, so I browse around and pick up all the free brochures and magazines in order to read something useful—like how to find those fancy houses and things to do while in a town. As I move towards the tall, glass refrigerator, I stop to look for Paw. He must be in the restroom—there's no sight of him. In a flash, I grab an ice-cold bottle of water and stick it between the papers. Pretty certain no one sees me.

"What in the hell are you're doing, Lady?"

I recognize the voice but don't see a body. Best to ignore the inquiry and pick up my pace but not too quick; don't want to look suspicious. Out of nowhere, a huge hand tugs at my collar. I wrestle with the papers and try to keep the bottle hidden. The moisture off the bottle makes the papers soggy, losing my grip it crashes to the floor, *splat!* and bursts open. The explosion splashes water, and throws glass everywhere, and the glop covers my shoes. I'm busted.

"Damn it, Lady, think you're going somewhere with that bottle?" Paw scolds.

The man comes around to see the mess.

"Seems my kid was headed to pay for this, and she dropped it."

No way I'm payin' for this since there's never any money. I'm perplexed over this statement.

"Give her a mop. She'll be glad to clean it up," he says jabbin' at my shoulder. Whoa, the mop is bigger and heavier than me.

"No need to make her do that. Accidents happen," says the attendant.

His kindness is greatly appreciated—by me more than Paw. From the ache in my shoulder, I know there's a plan. And, no one changes whatever it is.

"I insist," trying to control the decibels of his voice while keeping a chuck hold on me.

The man doesn't have a clue any moment could be his last if Paw doesn't get his way. Helpfulness—or any show of kindness—isn't something Paw handles well. Spasms are pulsating through my neck and shoulder. I refuse to cry.

Just when the day couldn't be any more bizarre, here comes Mama. No kiddin'. First, I thought it was one of those mirages—nope—she's standing there at the register, stroking her locket, and surveying the scene.

"What's taking you so long, Lady? Just what *is* your problem today?"

These questions are more rhetorical than a display of any real interest in sincere and truthful answers. Neither do I think she's lookin' to be helpful.

"Well, see, I was like . . . well, like trying to get . . .," I'm stammering to find an acceptable explanation. Mama, with hands on hips, glares at Paw and says,

"Oh hell. Pete, settle up with the man; Lady, get in the car this minute. I'm tired of waiting." She has spoken. She turns and sashays out, but not before flashing the attendant *the* grin.

Now you realize, of course, Mama never makes a scene in public, and as for bossin' Paw around, it's amazing' he takes it; therefore, this a monumental occurrence. I'm not sure Paw realizes what transpired. Of course, the man remains totally unaware of our family drama. Slumped over his mop bucket, he is ignorant to the fact Paw is making his way out, without payin' of course. The next zinger comes as soon as we're on the road, and he begins a lecture,

"Listen here. I don't want you to take something without payin' ever again. Understand?"

Holy crapolla. I think my ears need cleanin' 'cause this is the most absurd thing out of his mouth. After all, he's at his best when he's runnin' without payin'.

"It's wrong, just wrong to steal, and trust me, the consequences when you get caught, well, you just don't want to go there."

I'm flummoxed; totally.

"And, if I ever catch you again, I might just take you to an orphanage and never come back; I don't need anyone who's a thief. Family or not."

Is this speech supposed to be—what: Motivational? Inspirational? Intimidating? A serious threat? He looks in the rearview mirror to be sure I'm listening and continues,

"Look here, as long as you're livin' with me, if you *ever* engage in *any* dishonest activities, again you'll be hitchhiking the rest of your life. One more thing, it's about time you help with Mama and Scarlett O'Hara. That will keep you busy and out of trouble."

It's not a bad idea—assisting with the family even though they are really needy—and I'm only a kid. The hitchhiking part—really? *What-ever.*

"Yes sir!" I say with genuine enthusiasm.

Of course, I never steal anything, no matter what, again. Now, in spite of the pinches and nudges, I'm not afraid Paw will hurt me. His temper hasn't happened since the night Mama almost died with Scarlett O'Hara. I'm fearless—and often feel like I'm protected by something . . . can't always put my finger on it. I know to be respectful when Paw speaks—just in case the temper goes wilder than usual. With my good instincts, I can take care of myself, but Scarlett O'Hara and Mama need protectin', too.

#

We're on a rugged backroad when the Chevy goes *kaput*. Right there—not a person around—it stops. Paw should be able to fix it since that's what he does, but evidently Chevys aren't his expertise. So, we're stuck. We're sort of helpless with no idea about nothin'. Paw reassures Mama with a kiss and scrams down the endless road. Mama doesn't seem upset; Scarlett O'Hara is easily distracted with me telling her a made-up story, and it seems it's better to stay calm and carry on.

A few hours later, we hear a horrendous roar. A brown and yellow boxy form clamors in our direction. The long oversize front window resembles a giant, open mouth. When it gets closer, we can see the coffee-colored wood side panels. The contraption hacks as it moves along. No way we're gettin' out of the Chevy. After what seems like forever, the monstrosity comes to a stand-still. The lights are winkin' non-stop. *Guess who*?

He explains this car is a 'Woody' because of the wood panels. To me, it looks like a small house on wheels. The back is big enough for Sister and me to do a full body spread out, and there's room in the 'way back' for the tattered luggage. The wide rear window frames the countryside. The bass and tremble from the radio reverberates through the side panels. All this spaciousness will provide a better living arrangement than the Chevy.

He escorts Mama to the new front seat, and they lip-lock, a-gain. He tucks Scarlett O'Hara and me in, too. The interior is immaculate and hanging from the rearview mirror hangs a cardboard tree that makes the car smell like a pine tree: clean and refreshing. Only one small coil sneaks out of the cushion.

However, the best part, truly the happiest part, is the present for Mama on the seat.

"Happy Anniversary, Marilyn," he pronounces.

Now, in this family, holidays of any kind aren't celebrated. Don't know why, but that's the quirky rule. Right now, Paw exhibits some sentimental behavior. She plays with the ribbon on the package and gazes at him like…well, her face glows, and you can tell she really loves him. Anyway, I want her to tear into it since anything we get is most always covered in newspaper or cellophane, so this properly wrapped parcel with a ribbon is creating such glee—for me at least; I can hardly control myself.

"Hurry Mama, pleeeeease. Open it!" I plead.

She's the Prima Donna of Dawdle: No one does it better or more aggravating, which is about to drive me *in-sane*—until she finally pulls the purple string off and hands it to me. The paper falls off. I'm holdin' my breath and about to crush the life out of Scarlett O'Hara. She raises this exquisite, smoky-lizard handbag with a plastic handle. I try to touch it, but she covers it up. The whole thing is half the size of Scarlett O'Hara. On the leather, hanging by one microscopic screw, is a nametag. I strain my neck so I can read the letters, P-R-A-D-A. Mama fakes sniffles, and a utters a series of breathless: "Oh Pete." I don't know why all this drama since from where I sit, this is a pretty happy moment. Does actin' like this make it more special?

Taking stock of the day it, it's been awesome. We got a home on wheels, Mama's got an anniversary present, and I have a slick ribbon to share with Scarlett O'Hara. Being dramatic doesn't work for me. With two pencils, I do a rat-tat-tat drum roll on the door. This activity is hardly gonna bother the folks since they are too busy gettin' mushy and Sister seems to be in her own world. She's still mute, but I know she'll talk when she's inspired. Mama holds the P-R-A-D-A tighter than she ever held Scarlett O'Hara or me. Little did I know its significance or usefulness until much later.

Paw accelerates, we wave goodbye to the Chevy and depart. Can't even think about the variety of adventures waitin'. Randomly, once again, he is profound with,

"Sometimes, it's as important to know where you've been, so you can appreciate where you *are* when you get there." We'll see about that. Just sayin'.

CHAPTER FIVE

The Woody makes a great roaming home. Paw is flush with cash for right now, and each time we stop for gas, he buys plenty of Peanut Butter Crackers, Cheese Wiz, Mars bars, and salty, petrified, but delicious Slim Jim's—probably a zillion years old. He brings hot dogs, cooked in grease on hot rollers, and an assortment of donuts and cupcakes. Once in a while, he gets airy donut holes. One pop in the mouth, a few chews, and they're gone. The sugary, golden ones cover my lips with a sticky glaze. They're my favorite. Eating two at a time is greedy, so I savor each one; that way they'll last longer. At bedtime, we drink delicious, velvety chocolate milk; however, my insomnia is no better in the Woody. Paw enables Mama's addictions with fancy bottles of booze and a variety of cigarettes. There's no end to what he'll do for her even if it's detrimental to everyone's health.

It's a cozy night in a national forest. Fireflies swarm around the car. *Why do they glow?* A question worth askin' next time Paw has time to talk. The moonlight is creatin' skeleton silhouettes out of the trees, and the wind makes their arms swing in chaotic directions. It's entertaining rather than creepy. Besides, I'm brave like Paw. I push the subject of training to be a fixer, but he is adamant. "Why?" I nag. He explains it's a man's job and not an occupation for a lady. Seems a bit chauvinistic to me, but if that's the way he feels, that's that. I swear Scarlett O'Hara is sleep talking, but when I put my ear to her mouth, all I get is drool. Mama's body smothers Paw's like grilled cheese on white bread. His arms are locked around her. It would take a chisel to separate them. Their position seems uncomfortable to me. The P-R-A-D-A is at the bottom of her feet. If the world blew up right now, I know two people who wouldn't notice. It's a long shot, but just in case a disaster strikes, I remain vigilant and wait for sunrise.

Ambling along, Paw designates me the family tour guide. New pamphlets and circulars provide invaluable information. In the next town, I pick out a zoo.

"Hey Paw, would you look at this? There's a zoo in this town coming up. I think it would be a great idea if we went. Whad' ya think? Up for some lions, and tigers, and bears, and cotton candy?"

Mama turns up the radio, and he shows no interest in answering the question. I figure he needs a minute to think about it. I start to formulate my argument why we should go—in case he wants to debate. Here's my logic: We've been in the car for a few days without many stops; therefore, it's time for an excursion. I figure there's a 50/50 chance he'll go for it although—he always tells me, 50/50 are silly betting odds since you really never win big money. It's only the zoo, so I figure I can run with it. Sister and I are intelligent, in spite of bein' road-schooled: she can draw as good—if not better—than the graphic novel illustrators in books I see in stores. I can recite all the constellations, species of trees, read anything, and know every famous one-name actress or actor, Mama's contribution to our education—and math helps me win at Gin Rummy, Poker, "21", and Craps; however, we know zilch about animals. I crank up the ask and hold my ground. It appears there's a lot to see and do at a zoo.

"Can we go? Please, now?"

He stops the car.

"Show me what you're talking about."

I hand him the brochure. He flips it around—doubt he's reading. I don't care. He hasn't said no, yet.

"Lady, looks like this is your lucky day," he says.

He told me once he doesn't believe in luck. Claims a person becomes successful through experience. If he thinks it's my lucky day, fine with me.

"To the zoo," he announces with a bravado as if it's his idea.

I don't care who gets the credit. We're going.

#

Later, images of the animals run through my head: orangutans, Banded Gila Monsters, and a non-fire-spitting Komodo Dragon. Visions of slow moving, dried-up alligators and crocs with hungry jaws are destined to give me nightmares—if I ever sleep. Thought for certain Sister was going to let out a bone-chilling scream when the lion got so close, we could see his spit, but not. His ginormous mouth didn't upset her—not one bit. Makes me sad thinking how the mother chimp gathered her babies to feed them bananas. It was a heart-warming display of love and affection. Someday, I hope I'll understand why Mama is, well, Mama.

#

After this excursion, and for the first time, the entire family appears happy: he whistles, she hums, Sister draws precise, minute pictures of children playing, and I sway to the music on the radio. Everyone is content. Thinkin' this zoo trip might be enough to tempt Paw into giving serious consideration to settling down in this town—if only Mama would speak up and suggest it. Since my opinion has no merit—no reason to bring it up. Just have to be patient. Next day, we're off to our next stop—another excursion not without some excitement.

We're headed—who knows where—when the Woody is assaulted by a major rainstorm with blinding blue-white lightning and thunder claps so loud and close to the ground it shakes the car; the wipers are swishing back and forth so fast they're shooting water every which way and Paw, for the first time ever, has both hands on the wheel. Mama is composed given the circumstances, Scarlett O'Hara is napping, and I'm captivated by the downpour. Torrents of rain slap the sides of the car. Deep trenches overflow and each time the Woody speeds through one, the waves obliterate the windows. It's as though a giant surf is swallowing the vehicle. I want to ask Paw what makes thunder and lightning, but he has to concentrate. With my fingers on the seat, absent mindedly I'm keeping time to the ping, ping and wallop sounds of the rain. I forget this is an irritating distraction. Not Paw. He stomps on the brakes and right there in the middle of the biggest storm of my life, he turns and looks—the temper look, grips my hands, and shouts,

"LADY! Next stop I'm gonna tape those hands. And maybe your mouth so you won't be making any fuss." I swear he looks like he's about to have a brain pop.

Holy crap. I freeze. This is a distressin'. Mama doesn't say a word. With one hand, she strokes his leg, and the other caresses the locket. He stalls. Slowly inhales and exhales, returns to his previous disposition, and continues driving. It was the longest minute, and one I will remember my whole life. Mama is lookin' straight ahead, smilin' and shakin' her head like she's participating in an imaginary conversation. I'm stone for now.

When the downpour subsides, Paw replaces his arm around her. Sister is making raindrop circles on the windows. Carefully, I lower the window. The soaked fields of grass and wheat smell earthy, and the air is cool and crisp and tickles my skin. I stick my head all the way out the window. The humid breeze makes my hair a matted mess of kink.

Unexpectedly—smack in front of the car—is a rainbow. An arc of red, blue, yellow, and green stretches over the road and reaches beyond where we can see. Paw explains rainbows appear when raindrops reflect sunlight and turn the droplets into colors. He's so smart. He says prisms are like that, too, only I've never seen a prism.

"Would you look at that?" Paw says like he made it. "Here's an idea. Why don't we follow it and see where it goes? There's an old saying that at the end of a rainbow is a pot of gold. Let's see if that's true," he adds with a mischievous tone in his voice.

A pot of gold you say. We sure could use it. Now, most people know you really can't follow a rainbow, and there is no pot of gold, but Paw says it's so, and there's no contradictin'. We drive for a while, but it seems to move faster and further. It starts to fade.

"Hurry, or we'll never find the gold," I say, slightly freaked out.

He speeds up. We pursue and then out of the sky—framed in the front window—are blinding flashes of gold lights. When we're right under the display, we realize it's not a pot of gold but rather rods of fancy strobe lights outlining skyscraper high letters: BOONESVILLE–YOUR NEW HOMETOWN. A billboard displays a castle-size house, kids on swings, parents holding hands, front yards decorated with maple trees, and flowerbeds vibrant with flowers. I swear I can hear all the laughter, smell steaks sizzling on a grill, and feel the delicate blades of fresh cut grass in between my toes. We have got to live here, just got to. When Paw asks me,

"What do you think about this for our hometown, Lady?"

I can hardly believe he's consulting me, or suggesting this might be the place, so I hit the side of my head to be sure my ears get back on track.

"Are you really asking me?" while I wax pick.

I'm full of notions, but when it comes to Mama and her dreams, that's a serious, "no comment." At this point it's just better to go with whatever he's thinkin'—if you know what I mean. He's too impatient to wait for a response. Damn, my momentary hesitation caused me to miss a chance to speak my mind.

"Thought you'd have an opinion—since you don't—I think this looks like a fine place to stay."

And, there you have it. It's settled. I look at the sign again. Our hometown. At last: Booneseville, Mississippi, population, 2,954, but we'll add 4 more. We'll have it all: bikes, friends, bedrooms painted in rainbow colors, so we always remember how we got here, beds decorated with frilly covers topped with tons of pillows, play equipment in the yard, Mama's pool, lots of food, all flavors of ice cream and snacks, a melodic church bell that will chime at the top of the hour, and, most of all, a school. It's time for a brick school. We're not getting any younger and we're out-growing our present educational system primarily because Paw has fixin' to do, and Mama's not interested in any teachin' whats-so-ever. From where I sit (in the backseat, of course) this will make an ideal hometown. Paw pulls into traffic and heads to Boonesville. A whisper comes from the back seat,

"Home," and Scarlett O'Hara speaks for the first time.

I'd like to tell you we head straight to Boonesville, but Paw says I can't lie any more than I can steal, so, no, we don't. My gut feels all flippy-floppy—must be the stale Cheezy Puffs. Paw knows how to keep his family in suspense.

There's a lot of whispering going on—sure hope they'll include Scarlett O'Hara and me in whatever they're plotting. I can't *imagine;* however, I don't have to wait long for an answer. Instead of doin' what we're expectin', he finds an RV park and rolls the Woody into it. An RV park, really?

Now, our car doesn't exactly qualify as an RV, but the attendant lets him park for a small fee. On the property are miniature log cabins where we stay when Paw goes off fixin'. It's a like a pretend town without a fancy name. There's a playground and a pool with a high diving board. We take nice hot showers with so many bubbles we look like spooks. In the washer and dryer, I clean half our clothes at a time, so we're not naked. When he's around, Paw isn't social, but Mama behaves as though our impending movie life is getting closer to reality. Reclining in a canvas chair, she's silently animated, bobbing her head, watching and waving. Folks politely wave back like they know her. She's enthralled with the poolside parties and the adults drinking and smoking but she never joins the festivities. She's captivated by the children playing Tag or Hide-n-Seek. We don't participate. Just don't feel we fit in, I guess.

When Paw's away she doesn't get out of bed. Her habits consume her. Her stench is disgusting, and I wonder how he tolerates it. There's nothing proper—or ladylike—about stale cigarette or beer breath. These things will never touch my lips. I cross my fingers, hoping that once we have a home, Mama will cease this nasty stuff. Why won't he make her quit? Somedays, actually a lot of days, I just don't understand adults. Nothing I can do about it. In his absence, it's my job to keep everyone out of trouble and copacetic.

I wish I could take a break from worryin' and wonder if we'll ever be normal. The longer we stay here, the more I worry Paw's nervous energy will become a temper. These folks here certainly don't need to witness it because I'm sure if he has a spell, we'll be outta here, fast. True enough, one day, without an explanation and in a big huff, he loads up the Woody, and we're gone. Only this time it's because someone noticed Scarlett O'Hara.

See, she's what you'd call jaw-dropping gorgeous. She's only a kid—but heads turn when we walk around the park, and I'm sure it's not me or

Mama since her beauty is obscured under all the rumples and wrinkles, and my dark eyes and hair might be striking, but Scarlett O'Hara with her mop of twisted red hair, huge green eyes, pale, fragile skin, make people gawk. And her body is delicate, whereas mine, I think I'm still storin' a bit of what they call baby fat. And she knows when's she's got an admirer: She grins and waves. What else should she do? She doesn't talk. In addition, if being born beautiful wasn't enough, the person in charge of givin' people extra special traits was super generous with this artistic talent. Give her anything: cash register receipts, paper bags, or the butcher paper, when Paw can find it, and she'll draw a masterpiece. Once she found a piece of chalk and created a sidewalk mural that looked like the people in the RV park. It caused a buzz. People gathered around and chatted about its accuracy. But, when she's creating, there is no distracting her; therefore, one day, under a tree, engrossed in whatever her imagination is directing her to draw, a man approaches her. Paw—sitting with Mama—sees him and jogs over. The man is bent over observing her and doesn't notice Paw is about to breathe down his neck until he straightens up and practically bumps backwards into Paw.

"Help ya?" asks Paw.

"This your daughter?" replies the man.

"Who's askin', and what's it to you?" Paw lobs back sarcastically; his lack of social skills and the nosey man don't mix.

"Sorry to intrude, but I'm admiring her remarkable talent. I'm an art instructor at the community college and rarely—if ever—do I see such attention to detail, dimension, and depth from only a pencil and from someone so young. This technique takes years to develop. Her eye is sophisticated and mature. Who taught her? What art classes has she had? Whatever she's done so far—she should continue. I predict she'll enjoy quite a reputation and following."

I can tell by the frown on Paw's face he's not understandin' or givin' a flip about one damn word. Nor does he care, and most of all, he dislikes being interrogated. The man isn't finished.

"I'll give you $ 200 for the illustration over there," pointing to a picture of a random cityscape.

"No thanks, and I don't appreciate you bein' here."

Why he'd turn down money we need—I think he is looney, but no is no.

"Okay then. Sorry I asked. I'll be looking for her work in galleries. Good luck." His leaving is timely because I could tell by the way Paw's pacing, he's about to blow.

#

With this RV stopover, I hate to remind him he's told a little lie about heading to Boonseville and all, but we're on the road to find a home, again, so what difference does it make? Except, I can't get, no won't get, excited. Seein' is the only way I'm believin' anything he says, ever again. Apparently, something snapped in him—maybe it was the man and his prediction; maybe Paw felt threatened; maybe he wants us to go to school; maybe he's ready to quit traveling; however, I gotta believe the altercation with that man, motivated him. Who cares the reason, right? Any progress towards havin' a home is appreciated. We'll see. Just sayin'.

CHAPTER SIX

Here's what happens. For reasons only known to Paw, he decides to go off in another direction. Miles of highway, and trucks with eighteen wheels; generating such a turbulence it almost knocks the car off the road. Paw's in a hurry cause' the speed limit signs and the speedometer numbers don't match. At an exit, he swerves off the freeway, does a two-wheel turn, and brings the car to a whiplash stop. We bounce off the sides. No one says a word.

"Marilyn, I think it's time you learn how to drive," he declares, gets out, and stands by the driver's side.

What? Mama doesn't know how to drive? I guess I never considered this since Paw does it—nor did I ever think she'd be illiterate in this area; therefore, it might be a good idea—before we get a hometown, and she needs a car—she learns how to drive. But why now and here off of this congested highway? Another ridiculous decision.

Thankfully, there's no smoking in the car, but she continues to sip her beer. He gets irritated with her stalling. Heck, honey drips faster. Not sure how much patience he has left.

"Move over now!" he demands. Must be feeling testy if he's raisin' his voice to her. "Get behind the wheel immediately! I'm not asking one more time."

The dillydally continues. The more he demands, the more she's not moving. His face blows up red, and he begins to huff and snort like a bull in a fight. Mama is looking at him out of the corner of her eye while she caresses the locket, and waits. Like magic, a trance-like spell comes over him, and every angry bone in his body relaxes. He actually smiles. While he's transformin', she straightens out her dress and checks her makeup in the mirror, she assumes her place in the driver's seat. With her hands on the wheel, she looks at him as if to say, "I'm waiting." Paw slinks to her side, turns on the car, and instructs her to lightly push on the gas pedal and go. She rolls the Woody slowly into traffic.

To date, my experience with cars is only from the backseat or watching a commercial where a guy in a ground-hugging race car is going about 175 m.p.h. 'round a track. The disclaimer advises, *Do not try this at home*. Oh really? Paw's a good driver; however, Mama's inexperience is making me edgy. He's got to know what he's doing.

So far so good. He coaches her about the turn indicators, how to adjust all the mirrors, and when to change gears. He tells her to put a little more pressure on the pedal, and we start to keep speed with traffic. That is until she rams the accelerator to the floor, and the Woody blasts off. The erratic steering makes the car wobble. She darts in between vehicles and pushes them off the road. The car is hauling over ninety. Paw is imploring her to slow down. At this speed, if he tries to take control of the car, it might roll over or crash. She whizzes around the big trucks and passes cars so fast they become a blur. Parked in the left shoulder is a police car waiting for lawbreakers like her. He sees her zoom like a Lear jet, turns on the siren, and begins his pursuit. She thinks it's a game and goes faster. The highway havoc is incredible. Burly looking trucker men and car drivers are blowing their aggravating horns. It sounds like a band of elephants in heat. Everyone is shakin' a fist, shootin' the finger, or yellin' words I can't hear. A Corvette zigzags to avoid the Woody and lands in a ditch. Two cars side swipe each other while one ends up head on in traffic and the other does a multiple roll over. Pissed off drivers skid off the highway. The cop is hauling it, too.

Paw is ballistic and orders her to *slow it down* but she only goes faster. Then he shouts,

"WOMAN! you have *got* to slow down, pullover, and stop!"

And that's exactly what she does. Remember nobody calls her anything but Marilyn? When he calls her WOMAN, that does it. She lets up on the gas, starts turning the steering wheel so hard the car goes into a spin, careens to the edge of the highway, barely missing the concrete side arms by a skoosh. She slams on the brakes, throwing Sister's body on top of me.

I head butt the window. Ouch. Paw covers his face and I can see his knees shaking like he's got to pee. The cop stops just before crashing into our car.

The cussing becomes a vocabulary lesson. The howlin' and door slammin' rattles my insides. The officer lists the violations: no license, no insurance, fifty miles over the speed limit, beer breath, and jail. Wait. The cop's reprimand isn't the worst part.

Paw is marchin' up and down wringin' his hands and movin' farther from the car. Makes no sense to me. Mama is in trouble, and he should be defending like usual. A noise like a robot squawk comes over the cop's walkie-talkie, and the next thing, he and Paw are racing down the highway. But Paw is no athlete, and the cop easily apprehends him. They walk back to the Woody with Paw's arms pulled behind his back. The cop is digging him with his club forcing him to hustle.

Mama remains in the driver's seat, oddly undisturbed by Paw's dilemma. With her right foot, she kicks the P-R-A-D-A under the seat. The locket is wrapped around her hand.

"Don't you *dare* say a word about this purse to anyone," she snaps.

I'm blinkin' and twitchin' and tryin' not wriggle but, geez, I have no idea what to do. At least Scarlett O'Hara is mum. She hasn't spoken since the sign, and like Paw's temper, I'm not sure what prompts her to talk. Right now, she needs to keep quiet.

#

Much later, in the police station, Scarlett O'Hara and I eat chicken nuggets with honey mustard sauce courtesy of the wrecker driver who towed the

Woody and gave us a ride. The vehicle is parked in front of the building. Mama is chain smoking and stroking the locket. Poor Paw's behind bars.

She leans in, and in a hushed tone, says to slowly walk to the car, get in and don't move—no matter what. She removes the P-R-A-D-A from its hiding place and returns to the lobby, without giving me another instruction. Then, BAM! BOOM! And—smoke. Dense burn your throat, sting your eyes, choke you, smoke. People are scrambling out of the building, running in haphazard directions, and a riot ensues in the street. The cops try to curtail and separate the crowd but give up. Fire trucks and two ambulances arrive and first responders are everywhere. The situation would freak out most people—especially kids—but not me. I'm positive the folks are in control. Pandemonium follows this family; therefore, this is an ordinary day.

The hullabaloo is getting more frantic and the stink seeps into the Woody. We start rubbing our eyes, which makes them hurt, swell up, and turn crimson: Making Sister and me look like alien creatures with laser beams coming out of our eye sockets. I hand Sister a tissue to cover her mouth, but instead she lets out a goose honk sounding sneeze and looks around as if to ask, "Who made that noise?" I let her think it's an invisible friend.

More people are gathering, and I'm starting to wonder what's up, so I stretch my neck like a giraffe and peer over the bottom of the window. Through the smolder and crowd, they appear, arm in arm walking leisurely, the P-R-A-D-A dangling elegantly on her arm. Paw gallantly opens the passenger door for her, goes to the other side, gets in, starts the Woody, and with his best driving manners, carefully maneuvers his family out of the free-for-all. Mama is practically on Paw's lap, and I'm still confounded over the events. And, *do I* have questions; however, for years any questions are answered with, "That information is on a need-to-know basis, and you don't need to know." When the truth is revealed, it's devastating.

How my family can return to tranquility after an action film experience causes me to ponder our uniqueness. Or, I believe that anyway. Miles later, it's darling Scarlett O'Hara who manages to bring the family back to the moment when she asks,

"Are we there yet?"

Don't have the heart to tell her we're not even close; therefore, I reassure her with a, "Soon, yes, soon," which isn't a lie because things have to change soon. However, I doubt a psychic with a reliable crystal ball could have predicted our next adventure. Just sayin'.

CHAPTER SEVEN

After the jailbreak, he makes no attempt to go to Boonesville. We remain on secluded back roads, sleeping in the Woody and behaving like model citizens. Mama never drives again and fixin' is sporadic. After a nighttime dumpster dive, I have a soiled, smelly book to read and some outdated magazines. Sister continues to draw the most accurate pictures of places and people. A home is not discussed.

Paw tries to keep things light. He decides, one Thursday (I know it's Thursday because I heard it on the radio) in a town called Beauregard, we're going on an 'R & R'. Never heard of an 'R & R' or what it entails, but he seems determined to give his family this experience. Before he changes his mind, as he's prone to do, I immediately begin reciting the town's attributes and ascertain from the newspaper,

"There's a shopping mall with stores like Sears, K-Mart, and Woolworth's."

You can imagine we don't shop much except in emergencies like when I start outgrowing my clothes. I continue the verbal tour,

"Look at this. They've got a Denny's, What-a-Burger, a McDonald's, and a charming diner called The Blue Plate Special. Whoa, here's an ad for the place with dino-saurs, a butterfly exhibit, and a street called Art-tee-Suns," enunciating with my best phonetics. "Holy cow, here's a swanky horse track with races every day at 3:00."

My guess is we'll head to the track. Since racing forms have been part of my education, it might be time to personally check out the races. Wonder if he's preparing me to be a horse doctor? Instead, he drives to The Blue Plate Special. We enter the diner and approach the woman at the front door.

We're quite a sight. Paw looks sharp and smells minty; Mama still fits in her pageant dress, although it needs ironing, and the heavy perfume of lilacs covers up the stench of smoke and liquor. Scarlett O'Hara and me are scruffy but clean in the only skirts and blouses we own. In our condition, I'm certain the woman is going to refuse to seat us, but to my surprise, her warm, "Welcome, all y'all," relieves my anxiety—until she escorts us to a table in the middle of the main window, sets down the menus, and adds, "Thank you for coming," and returns to her front door post. Wow. I glance at Paw thinkin' he's gonna want another spot 'cause he doesn't like being the center of attention. No. Instead, he pulls out our chairs:

We sit properly: posture straight, napkins on laps, and no elbows on the table. We look like the all-American family. There's lots of chatter. People walk by without a glance in our direction. When the waiter comes, he is courteous and efficient.

The meal is a feast. Paw eats smoked bbq ribs smothered in a sticky, sweet brownish sauce. He uses a million napkins trying to keep his fingers and mouth from being smeared in sauce. There's a hunk of cornbread and goopy potato salad. In a bowl is a heap of hot greens—something called, collards. Mama's a finicky eater and pushes her salad of lettuce, tomatoes, cheese, and bacon from one side of the china bowl to the other. Scarlett O'Hara is doodling on an extra over-sized paper napkin but manages to finish a basket of miniature burgers, finger-thick fries, and a gargantuan mocha shake. Me, I decide to order fish sticks because I want to see what kind of fish is shaped like a stick. My dinner comes with coleslaw, green beans and hush puppies—another food phenomenon for me. It's yummmie. I stuff myself. We use our manners, "Please pass the ketchup, thank you Ma'am, Sir, and no thank you." Paw says no matter rich or poor, you need manners.

When it's time to pay, I get worried Paw will disappear. I hope not. We have been treated like the other guests. I want to come back. Hate to think they won't feed me again if he skips payin'. Instead he pulls out a roll of money and starts to count out the amount, and gives the door greeter a couple of bills, too.

"You be sure to come again real soon, ya hear," she says

I hold on to Sister. Lordy, Paw's actually doin' the right thing? And all this nice, nice from strangers? It's all too much for me. I must be dreamin'. He turns toward the street with the galleries, and we're off.

I have never in my life, and I think I'm about thirteen, seen so many different types of art: canvases full of overlapping triangles and circles, portraits of bored looking men and women in clunky, velvet chairs; cities overcrowded with mammoth structures; and crowds of people dining in outdoor cafés. My favorite paintings are the out of control, make no sense, abstract paintings. Scarlett O'Hara wants to touch the textures of the paints—some rough and raised like the topography of a 3-D map and others smooth as silk. She leaves nose and fingerprints on every gallery window we pass. Sitting on a bench, holding hands and exhibiting awkward PDA, our parents are uninterested in their surroundings. Good news—we never go to the track.

#

Other Thursdays, we visit museums and amusement parks with death-defying roller coasters, and dizzy-making bumper cars. At one amusement park Paw, wins big. He gets so many stuffed animals: giraffes, horses, teddy-bears, and kittens, they fill the backseat. Our first toys, and we're feeling special.

We listen to a concert in an outdoor amphitheater. The whitish full moon lights up the indigo sky. A quartet made up of a piano, drums, bass, and saxophone create rhythmic and upbeat music. After each song, the audience shows their appreciation by standing and clapping non-stop. Paw is mesmerized with the group.

"Jazz, Lady; this music is jazz. Miles Davis, I'm sure," snapping his fingers in time to the beat. I love the haphazardness of the music and enjoy watching him wave a stick like a band director.

Not all Thursdays are spent sightseeing. Some days, we find a nice, shady rest stop and have a picnic. Sort of odd, since most of our meals are eaten outside or in the Woody. On our nicest thread-bare blanket, he creates a lovely spread with a variety of snacks. Nothing fancy. Only little packages of cheese with penny-size crackers, bags of tiny carrots with a carton of spicy dip, and packages of sliced meats. Dessert's a box of raisins. For all the snack food we eat, he tries, once in a while, to bring healthier selections. He keeps the car running, so we can hear the radio. "Food is more delicious with music," is his latest bit of info.

During one picnic, we listen to Chubby Checker instruct listeners to, "Let's Twist Again," and Sister and I attempt to follow his loud and fast directions. We're twistin', spinnin', and flappin' our arms like giant condors in flight. We've got the beat but have no clue what we're doing. Onlookers are clapping—but surely not for our performance. When we finish, they whistle, which I accept as a compliment. The folks are intertwined in a slow dance. They have no rhythm.

I'm beginning to think we are destined to this roaming lifestyle until I die. Mama's map is decorated with squiggly lines. We've crossed the Mississippi River so often you can hardly see it on the map. The Gulf of Mexico sounds like a foreign country ocean, so it's blacked out. Seeing the Pacific or Atlantic Oceans will never happen because Mama's no longer interested in seein' the water. There's an endless variety of cities circled, but he seems to prefer small towns to big cities—which to me—would offer more opportunities for fixin'. I guess not. Still there's plenty of places he could consider. So why is he so picky? One day he brings me a notebook. Don't know why, but glad to have something else to do rather than just watch Mama poison herself and Sister stay lost in her head. I start a travel and food log, noting our various adventures. Maybe someday Scarlett O'Hara and I will collaborate on a book. Right now, I'm feelin' like we have no direction since we've been traversin' the country with no short-or long-term stops. Got to come up with my own plan if I'm gonna help Paw get this family settled.

On the radio, I heard prayin' helps. Of course, I don't know how. From what I can gather, it's like talkin' to someone who isn't there, but they can hear you, and whenever they feel like it, they send help, or not. In my opinion, we're overdo for a non-moving home; therefore, I decide to do this prayin' thing. Come on—how hard is it to find a billboard house? Evidently, for this family, pretty damn hard. Or, so it seems. Just sayin'.

CHAPTER EIGHT

When the Woody's brakes start to squeal, the engine sputters, the tires take turns losing air, and the radiator leaks; that's the end of fun Thursdays. I'm prayin' all the time, but who's ever listenin' isn't making life any easier.

He says it's for-tu-itous the Woody breaks down in Homer—Homer, Georgia—Population, 6,000, so says the city limits sign. The Chamber of Commerce book has a comprehensive list of: commercial establishments, schools, churches, a library, and houses of every shape and size. This town is picture-perfect. I cross my fingers Paw sees its potential, and we stay.

The first night while the Woody is being patched, we stay in a

SleepyTime Motel in a room with two beds. After sleeping on floors most of our lives, sharing a full-sized bed is a luxury. The room is spotless, and the beds are firm like a trampoline. We bounce to the ceiling. Plenty of cotton soft, puffy bathroom towels are folded and stacked in the cabinet. My nose gets lost in the baby powder smell. The television and the radio work, too. Off the lobby is a fast food kiosk with long sandwiches layered with meats and cheese. Paw gives Mama some money. He opens the P-R-A-D-A, pulls something out, kisses her and disappears.

Here's another oddity: I've never seen her use money, so my first inclination is to look around for coolers of beer and any machines or cabinets with cigarettes. There's both. Something tells me she'll buy those instead of necessities like food and milk. She's hanging on to the P-R-A-D-A with one hand and the wad of money in the other, and since no one, and I mean no one, *ever* holds the P-R-A-D-A, I need to gain possession of the bills.

"Mama, may I help you organize this money?" asking in my sweet and innocent tone.

I decide to give her a minute—to think about the proposition—before I physically rescue the cash. She throws all of it on the counter, walks out, and never asks for it. I stuff it in my pocket and hope when Paw comes back, he'll applaud my conscientiousness.

#

Three days later, he returns in a mile-long, orange convertible. The seats are black leather, and the tires have polished silver hubcaps; the top works because he shows off by raising and lowering it. Makes me laugh 'cause it looks like a spastic, bobbing mechanical arm. *Is this yet another roaming house? Wait and see. Wait and see.* When they finish getting reacquainted, he pinches my cheeks and gives Scarlett O'Hara a hug and then proceeds to give the announcement of a lifetime,

"We've got a *house,*" emphasizing '*house*' and acting all proud.

I don't ask questions but run to pay the bill. He's not going to bail on this one. Good thing I know how to save; the motel serves free breakfast; I split the sandwiches which makes leftovers for lunch and dinner. I learn to limit Mama's intake of her addictions without getting her all pissed off.

Mama is the first to settle in the new car. Scarlett O'Hara is engrossed in a sketch. When I scramble into the back, I notice a square, tan case with a bulky handle on the front seat. Looks like Paw's got his own P-R-A-D-A, only it's not as pretty. Can't wait to see if he's tellin' the truth. He's driving slower than usual. The anticipation has got me in a knot. If he's messin' with me, well, I just don't know what I'll do. *Please, please . . .Paw take us home. To a pretty home.*

He takes his time driving through Homer. Finally, we end up on a skinny, undeveloped, gravel path. We must be at the edge of nowhere 'cause there's nothin' around. Except—can't be? Is it . . . for real . . . our house? One lone, pole floodlight gives me only a partial view of . . . this . . . trailer. *Our home is a trailer? Homer is bad enough for a hometown name, but a trailer? Paw sure can pick 'em. How totally unglamorous. I must be having a nightmare or suffering from too many road fumes.*

Reality check. This is it. Paw carries Mama over the threshold; after all, this is their first home. I follow only to trip over the broken stoop. He'll have to fix it. Scarlett O'Hara is laggin' behind carryin' her art.

He immediately takes Mama to their bedroom and closes the door.

I'm standin', dumbfounded. Sure, it has a kitchen and another bedroom with broken-down beds and torn linens. There are two bathrooms, one in the large bedroom and the other in the narrow hall. The hall bath has a tub with deep crevices. Tar-like scum covers the sink and toilet. In the living room is a dreadful plaid couch. Feathers have escaped the cushions through fist-sized holes. The bird who gave his life for this atrocious piece of trashy furniture should get a medal. Deeply etched hearts with initials decorate a faux wood table surrounded by four wobbly chairs. Numerous windows are broken or the frames are empty. When I punch a switch, there's no overhead light. A solitary lamp with a crooked shade has a string and bulb. It works. The stained flowered wallpaper wilts off the walls. And, the floor has years of mud and stickiness. This is not like the movies, pictures, billboards, or anything of dreams.

Mad as hell, I storm out. Rage swells in my chest, and I kick a bag full of trash screaming out of disappointment and disgust but not from the crippling pain. Just because I'm only a kid doesn't mean I don't understand life. As far as I'm concerned, this is no place to live. Hell, the Woody was better. Now anything in my way becomes airborne: rocks, cans, sticks. Tears soak my shirt. I don't care. I pitch a rock at the tires and ball up my fists as if to hit . . . anything. Hold on! This is Paw's tantrum. *Calm down.* Collapsing into an exhausted heap of disillusionment, I wail,

"Hey you, listenin' to my prayers. Don't you *understand* what we need for a *home?*" Fruitless, fruitless; nobody's gonna hear me.

Scarlett O'Hara is standing in the doorway. Snatching her by the arm, I drag her down the path. We'll go back the way we came; we'll make our own home. I'll show the parents who's the responsible adult. We don't get far when she pulls away, stomps her feet, flails her fists, and declares in defiance,

"No! No! No! I'm not going to be homeless anymore. This is home."

And digs her heels in the ground and refuses to move. The girl has chutzpah and guess she's got a point. I'm only defeated for now.

Funny thing is, tonight in the trailer, falling asleep is easy, my gut doesn't ache, only my ears are working in case there's trouble. All that's outside is a cricket serenade.

I'm not convinced this is what Paw has in mind for a permanent living arrangement and want to believe this is just temporary. *What is he thinking? Could it be our house isn't ready yet?* It's not like he consults me; therefore, before I lose all my optimistic outlook, I better have ideas for a real home—in case he asks. To my surprise, I don't have to wait too long for answers. Just sayin.'

CHAPTER NINE

In the daylight, the trailer is more hideous. Paw buys cleaning supplies, drops them in the kitchen, and retreats to their room. Guess I'm a maid, too. I sweep up hordes of dust bunnies, throw out bug carcasses, and scrub until l my fingers and arms are numb. All this effort fails to improve its condition. Who lived like this?

I despise this place and don't feel guilty. To make it worse, I miss our other life: Thursdays, the Woody, gas station attendants who cheerfully give me directions, the repetitive sounds of the wheels, vast highways leading to glimpses of city life, sleeping under the stars, which is difficult to do here because I'm a smorgasbord for the fire ants and mosquitos. The folks remain in their room. If Scarlett O'Hara and I left in the middle of the night—never to return— we wouldn't be missed.

On the other hand, don't misunderstand me: I don't mean to sound totally unappreciative. It *is* an answer to my prayin'. Maybe give it some time? Only I don't feel like I've got time.

Weighing the pros and cons—with myself of course—about whether to pray or not to pray—concludin'—probably without prayin'—things might become more catastrophic, and should I cease prayin', it could result in punishment of infinite misery. Much to my dismay, it appears there's only one solution—gotta pray; therefore, I reconsider—only this time I'm askin' for something specific: home remodeling—nothing extreme: A couple of walls patched, consistently working utilities, reliable windows, and a front door on all hinges. *Will the right person hear me now?*

When Mama trips over a flipped-up floorboard—instead of fixin' it— Paw takes a crowbar and pulls up several more. This proves to be hazardous until I position the table and chairs over the hole. That night, I decide to reverse my prayin' approach: grateful and humble first, needy—but not too much—second. I decide to kneel, too. The floor is nothing but splinters, but if kneeling expedites the message, my knees can be sacrificed.

After the family is in bed, I situate myself and begin,

"I'm slightly grateful for what part you played in bringin' the family and me to this point. Here's the situation—I need more help. The list is long; however, for now, you and me need to concentrate on rehabbing this trailer before it falls down. If you can hear me now, would you let me know? Amen."

'Amen' appears to be what you say after a prayer—or that's what I heard on a church show once. I figure it can't hurt to add this as a sign of respect. When I finish, trying not to disturb her, I quietly slink into bed next to a sleeping Scarlett O'Hara. But unbeknown to me, she's not asleep at all, and damn, if she doesn't pat me on the butt and says,

"Nice job."

Rolls over, spoons me, and falls asleep. Geeeeez. Not sure this was the sign I was lookin' for; however, at least somebody is listenin'. Who else is out there? Just sayin'.

CHAPTER TEN

From all the splinters my knees look like porcupines, and they're black and blue and raw. Yet, I can't explain it, I just know it, any day now, there's an answer coming. One day, I decide to investigate the immediate area. Paw won't be back any time soon; he took his briefcase—a good sign he's got more work to do.

Close enough to be seen, but not too close to the trailer is a spectacular, truly spectacular, grey, wood-sided, billboard house with white shutters, a fully screened-in porch, wrap around windows, ample shade trees, and gardens. A massive chimney pokes out of the roof. There's more. Parked in the wide driveway is a fancy blue sedan, a dust covered maroon pick-up and a blind-your-eyes, yellow golf cart. *And, why aren't we living here?* Lost in staring, I nearly miss what looks like an abandoned shed further away from the house. Read in a book once, sheds can be ominous, scary, and dangerous. Can't believe everything you read. I forge on.

My legs get scratched walking through the high, uncut grass Who cares? When I get in front of it, the plastic siding is faded and woodpecker holes cover the door. Shingles are on the ground. Fallen branches and dried leaves make a drape over the doorway. One small window is slightly open, and the structure slants. I'm so excited I don't care if it's haunted. The shabby door is heavier than it looks, so it takes several shoves to make it wide enough to slide in and prop open to get some light. The decaying grass irritates my eyes and throat. It smells like rotten seaweed. *Gross.* Menacing spider webs fill the air space. My presence disturbs the birds, and they screech their displeasure. Weeds sneak in between the cracks in the floor. Same person responsible for the lack of upkeep in the trailer must have been negligent here.

After my eyes acclimate to the limited light, I see equipment: a riding lawn mower, a circular saw, two different sized ladders—one short and the other super tall, buckets, tape, tools, lots of tools: hammers, screwdrivers, pliers, screws, and nails. Containers of various types of cleaners line the wall. Under a pile of empty burlap sacks is a Red Flyer wagon. What a cool thing for Sister and me to use to pull each other or tote things from town, or just lounge in like it's our own convertible. Wonder why it got left behind? Got to check the equipment. The saw works but it sounds like a blender puréeing a rock. Its powerful jolt thrusts me into the ground— the blade whirling out of control and slashes its way through the dirt. I'm scrambling to pull the plug from the socket. This machine will be too violent to use. The lawn mower sounds like it's stuck in a gear and has flat wheels. More deafening noise. The gaseous fumes make me nauseous. Common sense tells me to get out quickly.

Spinning around, my exit is blocked by a portly built man with thinning hair, and a thick five o'clock shadow, dressed in a wrinkled tee-shirt, checkered shorts, and sneakers. A pipe hangs from the corner of his mouth. A Rottweiler the size of a pony —and without a leash—is next to him. The man dances from side to side blocking my escape. A hammer is on the bench, and I reach for it, but he does a fake lunge towards me, throwing me off balance; therefore, I forget the hammer and decide to take a chance, push him aside, and make a run for it. Doesn't work. He continues shifting side to side to impede my escape.

And he laughs—at me—struggling. A full belly, ho-ho-ho laugh. The monstrous dog walks away. He shakes his head and follows the animal. They head in the direction of the model home. When they've reached a safe distance, I shriek,

"Hey, Mister, *who are you?*"

When he doesn't answer, and getting pissed he's ignoring me, I start to run after him. Why I need to know who he is and why he wanted to scare me, I have no idea, but there's no turning back now. Paw says you shouldn't go looking for trouble or be the first to start a fight, and as long as the dog stays away from me, I figure I can handle the old man. When he reaches the house, he pauses.

"You're welcome to come in and have a soda," he offers casually.

What kind of pervert scares the crap out of a kid, walks away, and then asks if she wants a soda? Now, I'm more determined than ever to get details in spite of my over-active imagination which is-at-this-minute conjuring up grisly things: murder, rape, hanging, beating, arsenic. One of my instincts tells me to get out of there; the other feels okay to check him out. I go for the later. A display of manners and fearlessness might put him in his place.

"I'm not allowed to take things from strangers."

Another laugh. He's got a weird sense of humor.

"Okay, young lady, I'm James Coons and my dog is Butch. You live on my property, so actually we're not strangers. We're sort of neighbors. Maybe I should have been more hospitable and brought cookies and tea, but something told me to stay away. I'm kind of glad to see you."

Neighbors? Cookies and tea to the trailer? Kind of glad to see me? Are you kiddin' me? I'm flabbergasted. Regainin' my composure, I let him have it.

"First off, Mr. Coons, it was mean of you to frighten me in the shed and laugh at me. Second, my name is Lady, just Lady, no young in front of it and no name behind it. Third, if that's your trashed-out double wide, why is it such a gross mess and virtually uninhabitable?"

I know the last remark wasn't neighborly, but it's the truth. Since I have his undivided attention, I might as well hit him with all my opinions and questions.

"And, by the way, I don't drink soda, but thanks anyway. One more thing. What about your dog? Is he a killer or not? And, furthermore, how did my Paw happen to move to your property?"

"Quite curious, are you? Come, sit, I'll tell you what I suspect and know." A slow drag on his pipe creates a smoke halo over his head. He begins.

"A man I assume is your father drove by the trailer several times before you moved in. Now, it wasn't always a worthless, wretched place to live. Why did he come so often? Have no idea. Been planning to demolish it and sell the pieces for scrap. This is my land along with the housing development across the way. All of this property—and more—has been in my family for generations. Born here, raised here, and only left to go in the Army. The night I saw the light go on and the convertible in the front, I figured he must be a desperate man to move into that wreck. Out here, strangers don't come around and don't need any 'Private Property-No Trespassing' signs. From watching him come and go, thought he'd be gone soon. You don't get to be my age without learning behavior. And some people behave really strange. Each time I started to walk over he'd be on his way out. And always in a hurry. I figured no need to bother a man on a mission. There'll be a more convenient time to meet. After a while, gave up trying. Wasn't going to ask for money. That would be greedy of me. Now, you tell me it's your home. Who else lives with you? When I saw you go to the shed, I thought you were only snooping. Figured today would be a good time to resolve this. I'm not looking for any trouble. How in the world do you survive?" He waits for answers.

Mr. Coons listens politely while explain my family and our pedantic lifestyle, and the incident with Scarlett O'Hara, which got Paw to settle his family down. I leave out the part about people thinkin' we're gypsies and our nocturnal, impulsive departures.

"You tell quite a story. Is it true?" he queries with wide eyes.

"Sir, I don't lie ever. Swear (crossing my heart) to you every word is true and as real as me standing here. Someday, you'll meet Mama and Scarlett

O'Hara and see her remarkable drawings. I don't know if you'll meet Paw, like you noticed, he's gone a lot, but I'm glad to know you."

Can't waste any more time being friendly—time to mention the repairs.

"Now that we're on neighborly terms, do you think we can stay in it, and would you help me make it appropriate? I don't want you to go through tons of trouble, but it would be nice if some of the important things were repaired. I'll give you a list. Might have to ask Paw if it's okay if you help though. He's peculiar about anyone being around his family. I'll talk to him. If it means the trailer will be better for his family, I'm sure he'll be okay with you hangin' around.

"You're proposing a trailer makeover? Does it look like you'll be staying?"

"Here's the deal. I can't promise anything. That's up to Paw. Right now, he's busy, and I can only hope it means we'll be stayn' put. To be honest—there's nowhere to go. So, will you help me or not?"

He takes another drag on his pipe. The longer he takes to answer, the more I think I'm wasting my time. I just hope he doesn't laugh at me. He doesn't. Instead he says,

"I suppose we can have a project. Make a list and bring it back in a day or two; we'll make a plan."

"Are you gonna charge me?" I need to be clear on any financial obligations.

"No. Why would I do that? I like having neighbors."

Neighbors. Big improvement from being called gypsies. This little miracle is remarkable. Can't wait to tell Paw. I hope he'll be happy with my creative thinking and resourcefulness. But he still has some explainin' to do about how and why we're here. I hate bein' clueless when it comes to my family.

#

He's home. From the slammin' and stompin' in circles, I assume his last fixin' wasn't successful. Got to be careful how I approach this project. I know he'll want to be in control of the outcome so I have to be careful not to hurt his ego. On the other hand, there's never an opportunity for conferences; therefore, I'll have to dive in and give it my best.

"Hey, Paw, thank you for findin' this place. I know this is our first home and all, and we seem to be adjustin', but don't you think the place could use some fixin'? Ever give any thought to you and me working together to fix this up?" I mean, there are some obvious things that need repairin'."

Pretty bold of me. Just in case this question causes a tantrum, I move back a bit. The walls have become Swiss cheese. Now his marching sounds like a stampede.

"Where in the hell did you get that idea?"

"You know from brochures and catalogues. And, when we stayed at the motel there was this interesting television show about remodeling. Looks pretty easy to me."

"You think you're an expert?"

"No Sir!" I don't want him to think I'm a know-it-all because he goes ballistic when someone knows more than him.

"Just where ya gonna get all the equipment?"

This question gives me hope—tells me he agrees the trailer needs some work. I start to rattle off about the shed and its contents. I babble on about what we can do. No reaction: I offer to take him to the shed. No reaction. Maybe Sister will help. You'll do a fabulous job—I add—building up his self-confidence. No reaction. Time to shut up.

"No."

"What? *No?*" Challengin' the response. *"Are you sure?* Absolutely positive? Is this your final answer? Like—have you noticed the holes in the roof are so large there's a loud whistle when it's windy? The plumbing barely works, and the lights—half the time we have them, and the rest of the time we don't. Pleeeeease, reconsider?"

Begging is not beneath me—this is a dire situation. I know I should shut up but feeing invincible and confident, I continue.

"If you won't do it then I will." Bold-big, bad, incredibly bad and bold.

He bloats out his chest, crosses his arms over it, one foot starts the-tap-tap-louder and harder like the kitchen faucet drip. If his eyes were any bigger, they'd explode out of his forehead. He moves towards me and assumes a hitting stance. I crisscross my arms and spread my feet in to a 'V'. I scowl at him and do a double-dare glare although, I have no idea what I'll do if he strikes. The hands come up—but before he can strike, here's Mama. Stoned, she stumbles through the room, moving from chair to chair until she's right in his face. Hanging from one hand is the locket. She reaches for him.

"Peeeeete, please come back," beckoning in a weak voice. His hands drop as though he is a puppet and someone let go of his strings; however, his rant is not over,

"Damn it. If you're so damn informed, you do it. I

dime or help. And, don't ask for any. You figure it out.

follows Mama back to their room.

Saved by her again, but his anger frightens me more wi

episode. I'm sick of his tantrums, his irresponsibility and di

he's taught me to show no fear in times of adversity, and I ca

with the outbursts, but the thought he might hurt me, or Sca

or Mama is worrisome and I'm fed up. I hope he goes off soo

#

My wish comes true. The next day, Paw throws his briefcase

and shouts a goodbye without looking back. I can't wait to ret

shed, talk to Mr. Coons, and start the renovations. Got no id

clue how to proceed, but I know that's gonna change. Prayin' se

working although I don't want whoever is listenin' to think I'm o

it to get my way. I'm beginin' to think they're watchin' and listen

only they're selective about what they want me to have. Want to

them in person someday. Right now, Mr. Coons needs the list. Not

it bothers him or changes his mind. He reassures me it's all doable

humbled with my unending gratitude. No more worryin'. He does e

what he promises; with no waiting, deviations, or excuses. Everyt

is going to be fine. However, still don't know if Butch is a killer or

Don't have a minute to worry about *that*. He'll have to let me know w

he's ready to be friends. Mama probably won't care about any change

knowing Mr. Coons—but, Scarlett O'Hara, I know she's gonna want

be friends.

After the renovations the trailer is tolerable. He replaces the duct-ed window panes with slightly tinted glass, for privacy he says, and talls screens, so we can have fresh air with no bugs. Turbo stand-up s circulate cool air. The oaks hovering over the structure shelter the of from the blazing Georgia sun.

Scarlett O'Hara sits in the middle of all the commotion; Mama sleeps. hen we finish, Scarlett O'Hara tacks up a pencil sketch of our family front of a fancy trailer. She and I are sitting next to each other on orch steps, a man and his dog are off to the side, watching. The folks— raided together—are so far off in the distance, they're almost specs in the andscape. Is this a premonition? Time will tell. Just sayin'.

CHAPTER ELEVEN

When Paw is gone, Mr. Coons takes me in his pickup and we drive all over town. Scarlett O'Hara usually stays home; it takes a lot of convincing for her to go—she thinks I'm going to kidnap her—a thought that crosses my mind frequently; however, with a bribe to go to the park or the library or to buy more supplies, she'll go. Our outings are special. We joke and talk. Thankfully, Butch doesn't come.

Homer is in the middle, right in the middle of Georgia. It's so landlocked the closest water is Lake Mead. The town is a lovely place with tree-lined streets, and there's no litter anywhere. It bustles with people going to work, joggers, and shoppers. On corners, people visit. On school playgrounds, children toss balls and school buses patiently wait for them. It's not too far to walk downtown. Good thing because I don't always want to ask Mr. Coons for a ride. For sure, Paw would never be inclined to go.

The weather is one season: hot, shrivel-your skin-hot-kink your hair-hot-and ruin your clothes with armpit-stains-hot. At night, the temperature drops a bit. It's a welcome respite because shortly after sun-up, the thermometer registers another scorcher.

Off the main street is a park. The magnolia trees are heavy with delicate, lemon-scented flowers. There are rows and rows of roses, daffodils, majestic, standing-at-attention tulips, and borders of delicate, pale impatiens. Fat roots from a weeping willow tree swells the grass. All ages gather to play checkers, cards, or chess on the concrete tables and stools. Some folks rest, read, or nap in sloped style chairs. Today, it's just Scarlett O'Hara and me on a mission.

We meander. The sweet aroma of cinnamon invades my nose, and we follow the scent. Megan's Café is the most popular eatery around. People wait in line for her food and pies. Heard her food is as good as it smells and the pies are out-of-this-world. Makes it easy to understand why it's popular. We go in.

Waiting for our turn, I check out the way the waiters move through the dining room while effortlessly carrying massive trays covered with piles of plates laden with food. The pungent scent of rosemary and thyme drift from a platter of roasted chicken. In the kitchen, cooks dressed in double-breasted white coats and towering cylindrical hats chop and shake fry pans in sync across gas flames. Megan acknowledges her regular customers by name and chats as she takes them to a table. We don't want to wait, so we push through and take seats at the counter.

A nice waitress, in a starched uniform and hairnet, takes our order. We share an order of Mac and Cheese, two lemonades, so we don't die of thirst on the way home, and one piece of Megan's special peach pie covered in vanilla ice cream. I'm glad reading food magazines is educational 'cause it makes me food smart, and I can order with confidence. Mac and Cheese probably isn't considered gourmet, but when the dish arrives, it's magazine cover perfect: luscious, steamy, hot corkscrew noodles, thick with melted, golden cheese, fill the bowl. It's flippin' delicious, and we stuff our mouths until we look like we've swallowed colossal bubbles. By the time the pie comes, we're full, but no way are we're not gonna eat it. Not one crumb or one drop of ice cream is left. Megan knows what she's doing.

It's getting late. We hurry over to over to The Artist's Palette to buy more supplies: colored pencils, a heavy-duty sharpener, and as much paper as we can carry. Wish I had brought the wagon. The current free brochures are in a basket; I put some in our bag. I count out what's owed, and I'm one penny short. Panic sets in. I head in the direction of the cash register and the proprietor behind it. I'm so nervous tryin' to explain my problem,

"Sir, I'm one penny short and I'm not sure what to do. You see, my sister needs all these supplies. She draws because she doesn't speak, and well, her art is a way of communicating. If she can't draw, I don't know what will happen to her. Please, sir, may I bring you the money another day?"

"A penny you say? Don't fret. See this tray?" and points to a container full of coins next to the register. "Those are emergency pennies, and I'd say this is an emergency. Take one, and you can take your things and go on home."

"Thank you, thank you, thank you," being polite and obnoxious at the same time.

"By the way, next time you come, bring one of her drawings. We can hang it on the wall."

I'm so involved in payin' I fail to notice the walls are decorated with a selection of paintings, drawings and photographs. Sister's noticed, though. Spontaneously, in that damn beauty-queen arrogance, she turns to him and says demurely,

"Thank you for your interest. I will take it under consideration." Damn her.

Here I tell him she doesn't speak, and after he makes two helpful gestures, she says *that!* I'm horror-struck, embarrassed, and begin to apologize for her outburst.

"So sorry; Really I am. I didn't lie. She really doesn't talk. Oh my gosh, so sorry."

He's gracious with his reply, "No problem. I'll look forward to seeing you again. I've helped several people become famous. Would be happy if she was one too."

On the way out, she does her wave and grin. Why, oh, why does she do this to me?

#

She's quiet on the way home, but seizing the moment, I let her have it,

"Who do you think you are embarrassing me like that and don't you know we have to stay out of trouble, and you you you decide to pop off whenever you feel like it with no consideration whatsoever about what the other person is tryin' to do I don't get you at all sometimes I wish you didn't speak at all so I could keep things in order and then you go blahblahblah honestly you make me nutsy wavin' and grinnin' like you're important I don't know what but I can tell you this if you weren't my sister I'd trade you in for something useful. And, furthermore," I'm out of words and breath for the moment. She exasperates me.

About the minute I'm about to launch into the second attack, Mr. Coons pulls up and offers a ride. She's saved for now. I hardly have time to recover and she mouths off again,

"Mr. Coons this is quite gracious of you. I greatly appreciate your kindness and generosity. I'll repay your thoughtfulness when I'm famous."

Then, she does the smile and the wave. After this, I want a really big trade-in.

He drops us off at the end of the path in case Paw's home. He would consider Mr. Coons a stranger, and quite possibly, we'd be locked in the house for the rest of our lives. Or worse, move; a thought that gives me hiccups.

#

Never did get to finish lecturing her; at bedtime, she's sound asleep, or so I think, when she murmurs,

"I love you." Rolls over and starts to fake snoring.

What? *I love you*? In my life—so far—I've never heard anyone say those words. Come to think of it, I've never even heard a discussion about love.

Silly little pimples pop up all over my body. *Love . . . What does it mean? What or how should I think or feel? What does it look like? Does Paw love Mama because he tends to her and she does everything he wants? Are tempers love, too? Is going off and leaving your family love?* I'm stumped. *Wonder if Mr. Coons knows. Maybe the next time I see him he'll be willing to enlighten me? Hate to think I might be missing out on something wonderful. Or not.*

Words fail me, but I don't want to be rude and not acknowledge her,

"Okay," is all I can say.

Whatever this love thing is—is it contagious? Can't have Mama coughing more or another reason for Sister to stay all up in her head. Worryin' is my full-time job so is this love thing gonna take up my time? On top of all of this, right after this episode—I read in book about girls becoming women. Holy crap—like life isn't complicated enough and knowin' that almost any day we can become women when I hardly got any little girl time—all this for sure, is gonna give me extended insomnia. More than ever, we need some adult support and soon; therefore, until I get relief, I'll just pretend I never heard the words and keep life as usual. Or that's what I think. Leave it to Mama to turn me upside-down. Just sayin'.

CHAPTER TWELVE

I'm cleaning the cereal bowls when Mama shuffles in to the kitchen. Paw's away. Sorry to say I don't miss him. He's useless as far as I'm concerned. I mean, before he departs, he stocks the kitchen with beer, cigarettes and some food. Big deal. Deposits a little money. No hugs, nothing. Slams the door. He heralds his return with the constant annoying, sharp sound of the horn, barges in, and runs straight to their room. He emerges only to refill what Mama wants. I'm sure Mama is not cognizant of the day to day much less how long he's gone. But on a Walmart calendar, we mark his departure and his return. It only helps me keep life in order, otherwise, I really don't care. Wait. I digress. Back to the moment.

Unsteady and either hung-over, or already headed towards a bender,

she's pathetic. Off her boney shoulders hangs her *Miss New Albany State Fair* sash; the crown is surrounded by a pile of messy ringlets streaked with grey. The pageant frock is stained with beer slobber. She can hardly speak.

"I have . . . sur-prise for . . . you," she declares as she tries to sound sober.

Trust me when I say, "I have a shock for you," would have been more accurate.

"Come in my . . . roooom, and let's get star-ted. Hur…ry we have a lot to do," she stutters.

The room is disgusting. Ashtrays overflow with butts and mounds of beer bottles fill every corner. The P-R-A-D-A is on the bed and one of the suitcases stands against the wall. On the nightstand is their wedding photo in a dented frame. Match books from faraway places are in a cracked glass bowl. Souvenirs from Paw. The room reeks of sweat and sour socks. When Mama notices my grimace, she sprays the room with a lilac scented eau du toilet. The cheap fragrance makes it worse.

She opens a small case on the bed. Inside is a wardrobe we've never seen: one pastel shirtwaist dress, a cute wool sweater set with pearl buttons, a flimsy, short, white, lace and satin nighty, and low-heeled, slip-on slippers. Out of a camouflage bandana she unwraps her Queen heels, puts them on, rotates her feet clockwise and counterclockwise, kicks them off, and then rewraps them. She plops a straw bonnet with a fake carnation on her head only to yank it off and toss it back in the case, too. We're speechless watching this fashion show. She unzips an oval pink case.

"This . . . is my . . . making-up kit," she introduces this entity like it is a person. Inside the kit is a mirror and three shelves. The top shelf holds at least a dozen lipsticks in shimmering cranberry called, Kiss Me Crazy, and one lone tube of Candy Sweetness that looks like bubble gum. The case is also crammed with unopened packages of false eyelashes and containers of glitter eye shadow, tubes of mascara to lengthen, fill, and plump, round compacts of skin-toned foundation, and blush.

The second shelf holds a curling iron, hair dryer, comb, and scissors. A vial of hair goop has leaked on the brushes, and they are tacky.

On the bottom is the biggest surprise of all. Layers of jewelry. All the real deal; not the phony stuff. I can tell by the way it all shines. Extra-long, dainty, filigree dangle earrings touch my shoulder when I hold them to my ears; diamond studs the size of my knuckles, and bangle bracelets encrusted with topaz and tourmaline. There's a pile of long chain necklaces and a solid gold choker fastened with onyx. A cameo is attached to a plain ribbon choker, and an old-fashioned pocket watch has stopped at two o'clock. Entwined in the chain of the watch is the locket. The worn engraving is illegible, and when I go to open it, Mama grabs it, and returns it to its hiding place.

She slurs her words, "Now go . . .and get a . . .cha-cha-air . . and let's get starrr-ted. It's time . . . for Beauty Queen for a Day.

Wonder how many beers she's had this morning, but I overlook it. This is a rare event. Time to play along.

Scarlett O'Hara volunteers to go first. I'm not interested in the business of being a beauty queen or beauty in general. Besides, she looks like Mama, so her chances of winning a contest are better than mine. My hair has unruly, mind-of-your-own waves. I don't see curves on my body. I'm not what you'd call feminine but am not a tomboy either. A work in progress describes me best.

Like an artist, Mama begins to delicately apply the cosmetics. Each stroke of a brush, tap of a powder puff, or twirl of the curling iron turns Scarlett O'Hara into a glamorous young woman. When Mama places the crown on her head, and the sash down her body, there's Mama, all those years ago; without wrinkles, tangled hair, or the nicotine-stained teeth. On the other hand, her daughter, her clone and protégé, stands ready to inherit the title of *Miss New Albany State Fair*, or any other state fair queen for that matter.

My turn. It's gonna take two miracles; one to transform me, and the other to keep her alert. She applies the makeup with more flair. There's a tsunami of apprehension when she begins to snip my hair. I close my eyes. She works the comb through the waves and her fingers tiptoe through my scalp. She's never touched me this much before, and it feels heavenly. Then, she sprays a cloud of hair spray over my coiffure—gagging me back to reality. My patience is waning. Sitting still is hardly my thing much less having her fuss over me. Squirming, she raps me on my leg with the back of the hairbrush.

"Be still, damn it—just a few more minutes of behavin' won't kill you." When she hands me a mirror, I refuse to look.

"Ooo-pen your eyes," she orders.

Sister squeezes my hand; I return the gesture but don't know why. Is she warning me to be brave? Later, we decide a hand squeeze will be our signal something good is about to happen only right now, I'm not feelin' so good about this, or what might happen next.

"Look," says Scarlett O'Hara in a hushed voice.

My hair falls to the back of my neck in different lengths and straight bangs cover the forehead; cheek bones pop with mauve blush, and a hint of various shades of hazel shadow accentuate my eyes. My mascara covered lashes are fluffy and full like a feather duster. She's painted Raspberry Sweetness on my lips. It's a miracle, indeed.

Now oblivious to our presence, she carefully returns each cosmetic to their specific space and puts the jewels away. Sister removes the pageant accessories. Mama closes the chest and returns the making up kit to its hiding place. She's weak and tired. The stuttering is getting worse. She needs a drink and probably a smoke.

"We're fin . . . ished . . . bu . . . t you caa-can keep the makeup on for tooo-day. Wa-sh it off before you go to bed. It's never goo-od to sleee-p with a faaa-ce like that. Ruins your skin. Ma-akes you age."

This advice is out of character. Nurturing. Which she isn't.

"I lo—ve–you," she says, lights up, opens a beer, and tells me to close the door on our way out.

I'm so confused I don't know what to do. Mama's caught the "I love you" thing and I've got all this makeup on, and looking in the shard of mirror in the hall bath, I see someone I don't recognize. *Why didn't anyone ever tell me how pretty I look or how my hair shines and my eyes sparkle? How am I supposed to know all this is under my skin?* I'm happy and angry at the same time. Doesn't seem fair Scarlett O'Hara is a natural beauty. Why do I see *me* for the first time? And, this love stuff. Gonna need some explanation . . . and *now*. Hope Mr. Coons is home 'cause he's got to know.

I stare at myself for a long time. Scarlett O'Hara is sketching. Mr. Coons can't see me like this; I start to wash it off.

She declares, "You're so beautiful. Stop. One more minute please? I want to finish this picture. It will remind you of today."

"Hurry up. This was fun for you but not me. I'm so done with this silliness."

#

Running to his house, the drizzle slides down my scrubbed cheeks. Love, love, love. Got to get this right. His house and yard are lit up. Butch's bark sounds like he's ready to eat you alive but quits when he sees me. I know Mr. Coons is happy to see me: His moustache moves up and his lips look like an upside right banana.

"Good evening, Lady, what brings you over at this hour? Anything wrong in the trailer?"

There's plenty wrong over there but no time to discuss *that*. Once I understand this love thing, we can chat about trailer problems.

"Care for some tea? How about a snack?"

He keeps food ready. I know he doesn't get much company because there's no traffic down the path. He's always eager to feed me. The house holds the scent of cloves from his pipe. Butch stays vigilant at his master's feet.

"I'll take something to drink, but I'll hold off on the snack. I've got something really important and personal to talk to you about. I mean, really important," my voice near hysteria.

Don't know if he was married or has children; therefore, I'm not sure he'll know about love. Pictures on a table show him and Butch in different sized Jeeps and a jacked-up tank like truck. There are group photos in exotic places, but no one looks exclusive. My agitated condition doesn't seem to trouble him.

"Ask. I'll try to help."

"Can you tell me about love? Sister was the first to say, *I love you.* Earlier today, Mama said the same. These words, spoken specifically to me, are new. I'm like, totally, perplexed. I feel really stupid because I don't know anything about this '*I love you'* stuff. Do you?"

He sets his pipe down and pensively strokes his moustache. He's got to know, otherwise, I'm going to be ignorant the rest of my life.

"Over there. On the table is the Holy Bible; would you please bring it to me? I'm pretty sure there's a satisfactory explanation inside."

Fortunately, I know about the Holy Bible from the library; it's loaded with stories and inspiration. This must be a pretty serious question if he needs it.

When he gets to the section marked by a skinny ribbon, he adjusts his glasses and begins to read in a gentle but strong voice:

> *Love is patient, love is kind and is not jealous; love does not brag and is not arrogant, does not act unbecomingly; it does not seek its own, is not provoked, does not take into account a wrong suffered, does not rejoice in unrighteousness, but rejoices with the truth; bears all things, believes all things, hopes all things, endures all things.* He pauses.

This is a lot to follow. His fingers skip a few lines, and as though he's memorized the next part, he looks at me and begins,

Love never fails… But now faith, hope, and love remain; abide these three; but the greatest of these is love.

My eyes are closed tight while I think.

"Want me to repeat it?"

"Only the last sentence, please." This information has to be absorbed in small doses.

"But now faith, hope, and love remain; abide these all three, but the greatest of these is love."

I ask,

"Ok, so if love is all those things, and you need all those things to live, what does *love* feel like?"

"Lady, here's what I can tell you. A person can feel all the emotions: gratitude, joyfulness, sadness, fear, courage, weakness, strength, brilliance, stupidity, safety, and insecurity. Sometimes, it puts a knot in your stomach, and other times you, feel like butterflies are fluttering, and it makes you want to jump around. Love can make you feel omnipotent. How you behave and how others treat you—with kindness—that's love, too. Sometimes people don't know how to show love; they never learned, but they try anyway. It's hard to imagine bad things come from love, but it can happen. What's important is to forgive. That's the greatest part of love."

Yikes, this sounds like it's a way of being not a thing. Love is definitely contagious and complicated.

"So, when people say, '*I love you*,' do they say it because I make them feel all those ways? And, is everything forgivable?" I'm more confused than before.

"Could be. But what's important is—you are loved."

Wonder? How do tantrums fit into love? Probably should ask.

"But, what if someone—and I'm not sayin' who—does nice things some of the time but then gets cranky, and mean, and throws things, and yells for no reason, is that love, too?"

"Possibly. People get into situations, and they only know to act out: fight or flight, as they say. If they hurt or kill—there's no love in those actions unless the violence is used to protect. People sometimes do awful things because they believe the actions will make everything right."

"Mr. Coons, do you believe I can love someone?"

"Lady, you are the most lovable, loving, and forgiving person I've met. You're wise beyond your age. If you continue to go through life respectful, forgiving, and truthful, you will love many people and have a fan club who will love you back."

The rain is heavier and steady. Butch has his enormous head in the old man's lap. My insides are relaxed. One more question.

"Who wrote those words?"

"The Apostle Paul wrote it to the Corinthians."

Shrewd man—Apostle Paul and lucky for the Corinthians he shared his wisdom. I think about Sister and Mama and how they love me and now I know I love them back. Then there's Paw. Tough to love or forgive him— with or without a temper. Another attitude I'm gonna have to work on.

"Mr. Coons, is it okay if I love you, but I hold off a bit on loving Butch?"

"You bet! And Lady, if it's okay with you, I'd like to love you back," he says with a wink.

Relieved I don't have to worry about bein' ignorant about love, I can concentrate on pertinent family matters; the most important and immediate—school. Surely, this can be one activity we can accomplish without drama. *Who am I kiddin'?* Just sayin'.

CHAPTER THIRTEEN

For about a week, I observe the children across the way going to school. Seems pretty simple: The boys are dressed in khakis and knit shirts, and the girls wear short pleated skirts and cute button-up blouses. Massive bags full of books are strapped to their backs. It all is orderly when they stand in line for the bus. I knew it—this will be a snap.

One Monday, we pick out our cleanest and nicest outfits. Scarlett O'Hara wipes our shoes with a damp rag to get the dust off; we take turns brushing our hair, and when it's time to go, she packs a piece of paper and a pencil in a sack, and I add some money. I make two pb&j sandwiches and stick them in another sack. We hike across the field, get in line for the bus, and try to blend in. I'm friendly enough not to appear a snob, but I don't want to be super friendly with a lot of "Hi, y'all's!" When we board the bus, the driver, a tiny lady who can barely see over the steering wheel, drawls out in a booming voice, "Mornin', now sit yourselves down and be quiet!" Nobody pays attention. Every kid talks at the same time and several hop from seat to seat. They would never survive growing up in a car, that's for sure. Boy will I have stories to tell them once we're best friends. We sit in the middle of the bus so I can see ahead and behind. I hold Scarlett O'Hara's hands so she doesn't start her wave. Her grin is enough. I don't want to be too noticed, just yet.

Once there, everyone scatters to different rooms. Each area is labeled: Homeroom, Art, Science, Math, History, and Language Arts. The smell of grilled and fried food comes from the cafeteria. Lunch will be my favorite time for sure. A coach's bull horn blasts from the gymnasium. Teachers are scurrying around, and we follow one with a nametag, Mrs. Foster. When we're elbow to elbow, she says,

"Hurry along to your room before the bell, or you'll be tardy."

"I'm sorry, Mrs. Foster, but my sister and I are new here. We don't know where to go. Would you please help?"

If she starts asking a bunch of questions I can't answer, getting in school might go bust; therefore, for our plan to work, I will have to cooperate and give her as little, but as accurate information as I can.

"Well, what grades are you in?"

"I'm not sure, Ma'am. We *really* need to talk to someone about that."

The hallway is no place to divulge our dilemma.

"Let's talk to Principal Morton." We head to an office with his name all over the door. His secretary doesn't look up from her computer, but points to chairs and says,

"He'll be with you shortly. Please have a seat."

When he arrives, he's pleasant and not like movie principals who are usually gruff.

"Welcome to Homer Middle and High School. Let's start at the beginning. First, tell me your names and how you got here."

"I'm Lady, that's it; only Lady. This is my baby sister, Scarlett O'Hara. That's her whole first name. Got it? I think I'm fourteen, and she's thirteen. We don't celebrate birthdays like other kids because our parents don't commemorate. I like the fireworks and festivities of Fourth of July so I pretend that's my birthday. I keep track of my years by marking calendars. Scarlett O'Hara loves the lights, decorations, and music of Christmas, so that's what she picked. Our Paw insists on privacy, consequently I can't tell you his name but Mama is Marilyn; only Marilyn. We live on Mr. Coons' property. I promise we'll be in school, on time, every day. We won't be any trouble. We can do all the subjects; yes, yes, we can. You see, Mr. Morton, we've been road-schooled most of our lives. We're intelligent but need a formal education. Mama would be here but, she's laid up."

Obviously now would not be a good time to tell him about her deteriorating condition.

"And Paw travels."

He's frowning. I bet he thinks this is one enormous lie. Scarlett O'Hara hasn't said a word. Thank goodness. He calls in two teachers walking by. I guess he wants to see if they believe our story because, have to admit, it's a tad incredulous, to say the least. I must be a good story-teller because they ultimately find it plausible.

"Before we can place you in a grade, you have to be tested. The results will determine your subject levels. You'll be tested on vocabulary, math, geography, and science. We'll discuss your curriculums with your parents. Any questions?" asks one of them.

Parents. No way they're going to meet our parents. Never gonna happen. Better think fast.

"We need to be in a grade, quick. It would be better if we take the tests and get started with the work. We'll discuss all of this with our folks later. Right now, is just not a good time for a meeting." Getting really nervous but still trying to sound convincing. More discussion. At last a teacher breaks my rising trepidation and says,

"You'll be in separate rooms for the tests, and we'll send home paperwork for your folks to sign."

Separate rooms? We've never been separated; ever; for any reason. Perspiration drips over my nose. My brain hurts, and any excuse escapes me as to why we have to stay together. Scarlett O'Hara squeezes my hand. Separate rooms it is.

The tests are intense, and the questions give me vertigo. The big clock ticks off the minutes, hours. I wonder how Sister is managing. When a bell rings, a teacher comes to retrieve the papers. The others return with Mr. Morton and Scarlett O'Hara. They flip through the booklets and talk amongst themselves. Then he inquires,

"Are you sure you've never been to school?"

"Yes sir, I'm sure. We don't fib."

Whisper, whisper, whisper. Is this all teachers do is whisper?

"Lady, you and your sister scored higher on these tests than the district average. Your scores indicate you should be in advanced grades and subjects, but we think it's best to start you where you belong—you in ninth grade and Scarlett O'Hara in eighth. Once you adjust, we'll move you to the AP classes. One more thing, does Scarlett O'Hara need a hearing test?"

What? A hearing test for her?

"No Sir, no hearing test necessary. I can hear fine. I only speak when there's something relevant to disclose. What else would you like to know?" There she goes again.

The outburst is rude. I commence with an apology, but pause when she moves a chair to the whiteboard and stands on it. She takes a marker and immediately draws a caricature of the trio. Satisfied with her creation, she flashes them the smile and does the wave. What a flippin' first impression. We're either gonna be in or out. I'm thinkin' we're banned. Instead, they let out nervous chuckles. In a flash though, it gets serious again when they proceed to pile on schedules, books, assignments, and those damn parental papers. We did it!

#

Walking home, I'm trying to figure out how to get the papers signed. There's so much to tell them. Paw's just got to sign. What a remarkable day. I want our parents to be proud. As for her insolence: We're in school; maybe someone else can teach her what I can't. When I see his car parked in front, I get excited—but become majorly spooked when an ebony-colored car, the length of the trailer, slowly comes down the road. I pull

Sister behind a tree. Paw waits in front—his arms hanging at his sides, and his shoulders hunched over. The car screeches to a halt and a hefty man in an ill-fitting suit exits and starts hollerin' and shakin' a fist at Paw. Two other equally ornery looking men get out but stand by the car. Each man is playin' with something in his pocket but it's hard to determine what it is from our hiding place. The ugliest man starts yakkin' at Paw, but the idling car covers the words. Paw just nods. And nods some more. Kicks some dirt and nods. Straightens up and opens his mouth to speak but only nods. And when the screaming man has said his last word, they all get back in the car and speed away, causing a dust storm. Paw goes inside.

"Let's rest a minute and enjoy being here," I tell her.

From his posture, and prior experience with his moods, staying out of sight is best.

#

Sure enough. The kitchen wall has new holes and several of the windows are smashed. Our home is semi-trashed. The day's show and tell will have to wait. Their room is quiet. There's no smoke sneaking out from under the door and no radio. Later that evening, when I get up for water, sobs—real, hysterical, can't stop sobs, come from their room, and I can hear Paw, repeating,

"Don't worry. Things will be all right. I promise; I won't let anything happen to this family or me. Please trust me." Mama's staccato sobs get louder. "I have to do this, Marilyn, please try to understand. I promise."

The next wail could crack the sound barrier. Tonight, there'll be no sleep. Paw knows some strange people, and by his posture, fixin' must be getting really hazardous. I wish we could talk about family things like we do with Mr. Coons. There's so much I don't understand and probably could be a bigger help if I had more knowledge. I place the papers on the table and retreat to our room. It's past midnight when I see Paw get in his car and leave. I dash to check on Mama. Through the battered door—like a CD stuck on a track—Mama's feeble voice chants,

"Yes, it's going to be all right. It's going to be all right. I promise. I promise."

I rattle the doorknob—it's bolted; sitting on the floor, I wait to see if she'll let me in. The chanting ceases; scared she's dead, I shake the handle harder. The light goes off and smoke drifts out.

#

The early morning sun casts layers of burnt orange over the roofs of the houses across the way and heats up the trailer. Butch is barking—probably at a squirrel. Still on the couch, and fatigued from lack of sleep, I start to roll over when—holy crap, we have to go to school! I rush to wake up Scarlett O'Hara who's dressed and looking at me as if to say, "And, why aren't you ready?" In the bathroom, I splash water on my face, comb my knotted hair, brush my sticky teeth, get dressed, and grab the books off the kitchen table. The parental papers fall off the books. Damn it. I don't have time to deal with this. After I promised we'd be good students, there's no way we're gonna be late, especially on our first official day of school. Hastily picking up the papers, and about to shove them back in a book, I notice on the bottom line written in childlike, block letters, Pete and Marilyn. And if that isn't enough, on the three-legged chair sits a paper sack. I look, inside—there's money and lots of it. *What the . . . ?* Hard to ignore this bounty, but under the circumstances, the hell with it. We've got to hurry or we'll miss the bus. Scarlett O'Hara orders me to move it. Just once, I want our lives to be simple. Just once.

#

School is more difficult than I imagined. The days are filled with: book reports, tests, debates, presentations, and tedious homework. I'm studious but not a brainiac. Far as I'm concerned, the B's are fine. I'm thrilled when I ace New Life Skills—especially the culinary part. Teacher says I'm a natural with food. During Friday night football, we cheer until we sound like we've been sucking helium. Sister, on the other hand, has a photogenic memory and never studies. Never. In class, her hand waves constantly, and she thrives on answering questions with complex, genius-level answers and offers astounding and precise details that stun her teachers. She's inducted into the Honor Society and is elected President of the Art Club. Her talent has matured and 'First Place-Best of Show' blue ribbons hang from most of her work. Her reputation becomes state-wide. Mr. Sims, her art teacher, tutors her after school. At a garage sale, we buy a trunk to store all her work. There are only so many walls in the trailer, and the art supply store sells them so quickly she needs a backup supply. Everyone encourages her to apply for a scholarship to the Art Institute or Brandeis. She's non-committal about her future.

In order to maintain the appearance of being a family, Mr. Coons becomes our surrogate parent. He attends PTO meetings, school functions, conferences, and chaperones field trips. When teachers push to have meetings, the excuse is the same: Mama is indisposed and Paw is away. All the truth. They accept Mr. Coons as our guardian, and I don't tell them differently. It's better to let them think that way. Sometimes when we're together, his face takes on a sad, faraway, contemplative look—like he's remembering something; however, give him a minute, and he'll boast like we're kin. Makes my cheeks hot. Scarlett O'Hara grins and waves when he brags. Once I noticed him staring at her, I swore there was a tear on his cheek. Nay, it had to be sweat. Why would he be crying over her?

We're sociable at school but bring no one home. Mr. Coons offers his house, but we don't want to impose. One day, he gives me a blue cell phone. "What I'm supposed to do with this?" "It's for emergencies," he says, and programs three numbers: the school, his number, and 9-1-1. He tells me to keep it in my pocket at all times. What would we do without him?

The weeks zoom by. Paw returns infrequently without making a scene and thankfully never asks about the money—or our lives in general. Mama—I know if Mr. Coons saw her, he'd be mortified and insist she go to a hospital. She's nothing more than a skeleton with sunken eyes, a yellowish complexion, and a mass of raggedy, unwashed hair. We hardly see her, and she gets out of control when we try. Isolated in her room, the only signs of life: the chanting and smoke. We put trays of food at her door—it rots. What else can I do? I know I need to be more attentive, but how? Paw will *kill* me if anything happens to her. One night, while reciting my prayer: "*Would you please let her hang on until there's a school break? I'll work hard to get her well then. Amen.*"—the trailer begins to shake and pictures fall. *Now what*? Just sayin'.

CHAPTER FOURTEEN

Without warning, thunder vibrates the earth, and the skies let loose a torrent of rain. Emergency sirens pierce the quiet night. In the distance, a funnel cloud is rapidly making its way to the vulnerable subdivision: it sounds like a runaway locomotive as it spins ferociously while sucking up everything in its way. It will only take seconds for the tempest to demolish or diminish, creating widespread devastation. A second is the difference between life or death.

The vibrations wake Scarlett O'Hara and she runs towards the living room. I intercept her and scream at her to hide in the bathtub. Mama— holy crap—I've got to move her. The noise is deafening, and I know the trailer can't withstand the pounding. I kick in her bedroom door and start to lift her off the bed. Her anorexic body is heavier than expected, but I refuse to put her down. Like a petulant child, she hits me and yells,

"YOU can't save me. I don't want you here. GO!"

"Please Mama . . ."

"No, damn it. Get. Out. NOW!"

Scarlett O'Hara yells, "Lady, it's almost here! Hurry."

Mama starts punching and kicking me. There's no other choice. Scarlett O'Hara is panic-stricken, and Mama is uncontrollable. I slam the door, rush to the bathtub, and climb in next to Scarlett O'Hara. She's droning incoherent jabber; my heart is beating in triple time. We're terrified and hold each other. Then, with a force like a monster-sized washer on spin cycle, the tornado whirls and tosses the structure. Sister goes mute and limp. My stomach is up to my ears. I'm too petrified to ask for a miracle.

When the trailer is quiet, my first inclination is to pinch myself to check for life and then gently shake Scarlett O'Hara. She's holding her arm, and the distressed expression on her face alarms me, but she appears unhurt. Once on our feet, we dash through the slush to reach Mama. Her room is in its usual disarray, inexplicably untouched from the storm. Her complexion is now colorless, but her lips, damn if they aren't covered in fresh lipstick. She's hardly breathing, and when I pick up her emaciated hand, it drops on my leg. Her eyes are open and her head flops to one side. Lightly massaging her face, I beg,

"Mama, Mama, stay with me. Please!" Nothing; not even a groan.

"Run, go find Mr. Coons!" I shriek at Sister.

The cell phone is inoperable and I haven't looked to see if his house survived. "RUN!" I screech as she bolts. There's a chill to Mama's body; I hold her closer.

"Wake up; please don't die," pleading and trying to keep myself together.

The death rattle overcomes her entire body then her breathing fades—to nothing. I don't, can't, won't let go.

Mr. Coons and Sister blast through the hole where the front door hung, tossed like a Frisbee, and sitting on the land across the road. Mama and I are conjoined.

"She's dead."

Sister falls on top. Mr. Coons kneels next to the bed. Transfixed, he takes his arthritic fingers and lovingly begins to outline her face: her lined forehead; he gently lowers her eyelids—still open with the death gaze—traces the curve of her nose, and the hollows of her sunken cheekbones, tickles her chin, and stares at the painted lips. He holds her hands, then tenderly fondles her stray curls. He pauses and glances back and forth at mother and daughters. Without a word, for the first time, he takes Sister and me, and we huddle . . . tight, really tight, for a really long time.

#

The aftermath of a tornado brings shock, denial; and, when reality sets in, survivors grieve over lost relationships and possessions. It's macabre and surreal. Salvador Dali, surreal. The rubble looks like chopsticks; cars stripped down are stacked in haphazard piles. The storm is indiscriminate. One house is intact; the next one just a foundation. Household belongings are strewn for miles. Home and business owners are inconsolable. Helicopters hover over accessing the damage; a makeshift triage occupies the Community Center. The slightly injured are treated on the spot, the more seriously hurt are ferried to hospitals. The dead are slowly and respectfully removed. All of this activity is executed like a pantomime.

Mr. Coons takes charge of the funeral arrangements and buys a bronze urn for her ashes. There's no ceremony. I don't want our school friends to know. Besides, all the churches and undertakers are swamped with tornado casualties more important than her.

Paw hasn't been home in weeks. I know I'm dead—dead—once he returns. I doubt he'll forgive me for not saving her. Too bad. He wasn't here. How would he know how bad it was? Sister mopes and insists on sleeping in Mama's bed. We grieve without talking. Her drawings become abstract charcoal scribbles and when she's finished, she either burns or shreds them. When I try to stop or comfort her, she becomes vicious. Red ink covers her arms. As for me; some days all I want to do is curl up on someone's lap. Other and most days, I know Mama isn't suffering anymore: I'm sad, but peaceful. Most of all I wish I had someone to lean on, a shoulder to cry on, and a hug.

The fire marshal and Mr. Coons deem the double-wide uninhabitable and tell me it must be demolished.

"No," I beg, "you can't do that." Relentlessly, I plead, *"Please*, only fix it. We can't move. We have to be here when Paw returns. I don't care if it's patched with super glue, duct tape, and rusty nails. Fix the front. Board up the back. Replace the roof. Clean inside and be done."

"No. I have to do what the law requires and what's best for you, too."

Tearin' it down and movin' are no good solutions as far as I'm concerned. But after he sees my angst, he offers a compromise.

"If you insist on staying here and this is my property, I'll remodel it my way. If your Paw gives you any trouble—I'll deal with him."

I'd rather have Paw kill me than let the two of them have a conversation. I remember Mama's chanting. It's time for things to start bein' all right.

#

When he's done with the extreme make-over, the reinforced structure has new siding, windows, and a sturdy roof. He builds a porch and hangs a swing. We paint the front door sky blue. New appliances and furniture get delivered, and the colorful wallpaper covers the new sheetrock. A walnut bedroom suite fills our room and cotton curtains hang on every window. Central air conditioning and heat are installed. Mr. Coons buys a big screen television and computers for homework. I won't allow anyone in their bedroom, so I patch the broken window and leave everything as it was the day she died, setting the P-R-A-D-A on her side of the bed and standing the other suitcases in the corner. We don't dare open them. Hopefully, one day Paw will do it. The urn sits on the nightstand. If only the folks could see our home now. It may not be a billboard house, but it makes a terrific advertisement for trailer living.

Scarlett O'Hara doesn't want to go to school. Mr. Coons says she's grieving and will go when she's ready. Every day I bring home the assignments, and deliver the finished work to her teachers.

#

Several weeks after Mama died, a maroon SUV with 'Homer I.S.D. Department of Truancy' stenciled on both sides skulks up to the trailer. A chubby man in a too small suit and a lanky, matronly looking woman with hair in a bun disembark, stand and eyeball our home. She carries a clipboard and a camera hangs off his neck. Butch is fetching a stick but growls as they approach. Today is not the day for him to become a killer. Scarlett O'Hara is inside. The teachers have been tolerant of her absence, and she continues to surpass her classmates in grades. I can't fathom why they're here. They snub me as they make their way to the front door. This is our home, and they're trespassing. I bet they want an adult. I stick my body between them and the trailer.

"Miss, I'm Mr. Wiggins, and this is Truancy Deputy Hosworth." A deputy for truants, *that's* impressive. "Are your parents home?"

"So very nice to meet you. My name is Lady, not Miss, if you please. Mama's gone, and Paw isn't home."

I don't know if they think gone refers to her being dead or out shopping like other Mamas. I can tell they're pondering this because Deputy Hosworth clears her throat, stretches another inch, and makes a note on her paper.

"What's this about?" trying to remain polite.

"We want an adult. When will your folks return?"

Time to get creative.

"Well, I'm not sure. My Paw is an important man and is away most of the time. We *are* expecting him any day now. Like I said, Mama's indisposed."

Totally true. After all *he* could return *any* moment. I start shuffling my feet. I'm not accustomed to snotty authority . . . or authority period. Perhaps they'll give up and go. I see Scarlett O'Hara peeking through the curtains. I have to ask,

"Are you here because my sister hasn't been to school? You *do* know she contributes her homework in a timely manner and receives commendations for excellence? I haven't missed but a few days. Do you think we're delinquents in some way? Do you have to make a report or assign some kind of detention? Don't I look responsible enough to relay the message to an adult? *What* is the *issue* here?"

I hope they are impressed with my self-confidence and don't think I'm being disrespectful and they see there are no issues here, and, most of all, they're wasting their time. But I think in order to gain the upper hand, I need to give them a straight answer on Mama's whereabouts. I only hope it doesn't backfire and they drag Sister and me to Social Services or some shelter, or, a foster home.

"Just so you know, my Mama is dead." Their jaws drop so wide I can see gold spots in their back teeth.

"Goodness, now this is a problem. Who takes care of you?"

"I do. Been doing it my whole life. Even when our parents are around, I'm still the caregiver and adult, so to speak. Besides, there's Mr. Coons over there," pointing in the direction of his house. "He's our best friend and available when needed."

"What do you do for money?"

I think this is an irrelevant question, but I sense they are trying to grasp how we live.

"I don't know what that has to do with school, but I can tell you that my sister sells her sketches, our Paw works, and I'm going to start a part-time job soon. We have everything we need, always have, always will."

Don't want to share the years we spent on the road. They would flip out. The Deputy can't write fast enough. Mr. Wiggins is unsure what to photograph. I'm bored with this and turn my attention to a robin chirping on the telephone wire. All heads swing to the left when we hear tires tearing up the path heading towards the trailer at breakneck speed. Here comes the same ebony-colored car. When it skids to a stop, Paw emerges from the back seat. They watch him, limping, with his left arm in a sling. More on the job injuries, I suppose. Before they speak, he juts out his other hand,

"How do you do, I'm Pete, their father. Look here, I can assure you my daughters will answer to any incident caused by their misconduct. This will be addressed immediately."

I notice he fails to mention his last name. The woman scribbles more notes. She does another 180 look-and-see over our home, pauses at the car, stares back at Paw. Can only imagine what she'd like to ask but doesn't. I know they're finished. But it's not over yet. At this most inopportune time, Scarlett O'Hara makes an appearance. She walks over to Paw, loops her arm through his, and extends a truly mind-boggling invitation,

"Lunch is ready. Please come in and join us."

Are you kidding me? Lunch with *these* people? She's delusional. They look at each other like they might consider it. I get itchy waiting for their reply.

"We need to check on other truants. Thank you anyway."

Then Scarlett O'Hara blurts out, "*Tru-ants*? Who are you calling *tru-ants*? Nobody calls anyone in this family names."

Man, one of these days . . . hope they didn't hear *that*. Paw's eyes are rolling around in his head—left to right, right to left, at me, at them, at the car, at the trailer. He looks like a zombie. The pair can't gather their things fast enough. Surely when their bosses read their report, they'll find it so unbelievable, they'll throw it away.

"Just to let you know. A report will be sent to your school. Moving forward, we expect consistent school attendance, appropriate behavior, and good performance. If we come out here again, we'll have to take custody action."

Once again, our weirdness saves the day. This threat sounds reasonable but I know they'll never be on this property again. After hand-shaking with Paw, Scarlett O'Hara, and me, they vamoose. Another victory!

Ignoring the waiting car, he quietly says,

"Let's eat."

Unfortunately, once inside there's no discussion or a congenial lunch. There's a bruise under one eye, his clothes are two sizes too big and there are no more bulging muscles. His hair is platinum, and he looks like an Albino. Crow's feet dance on his face. The men rev up the engine. It's obvious they're in a rush. I know my time to talk is limited and I have got to—just got—to tell him what's been happening. I start blabbing and follow him to their room, but stop at the door. I continue speaking, trying to hit the high points in case he's listening. Shortly, he comes out with the urn.

One of the men shouts, "Get your ass out here, Fratelli." Paw disregards the order.

The other man yells, "Ya gonna make me come and get you?"

He shrugs his shoulders and moves to go outside. On the last step, he turns and says,

"Everything is going to be all right. I promise. You'll see. A Fratelli always keeps a promise."

We watch in disbelief. He doesn't even look over his shoulder at his daughters. Scarlett O'Hara starts to wave but I hold her hand down. The windows are opaque—he can't wave back. Chances are he doesn't care anyway.

Unexpectedly, Paw leaps out of the vehicle and sprints back. The driver puts the car in reverse and speeds up. We watch in shock—our Paw about to be run over by a mechanical assassin— right here. I can't bear to look. But no. He tucks and rolls and does a somersault like a stunt man, avoiding the motorized killer. He jumps up, and shouts as loud as he can,

"I prom-isssss!! I................," his mouth muzzled as they stuff him back in the car.

In a split second there's no trace of them. Sister drops. I'm brain and heart dead: I don't feel and can't think.

"He's never coming back, is he?"

Wish I could tell her—yes, he will—but, I don't want to give her false expectations. From the looks of things, all I can say is,

"I doubt it."

How was I to know his covert behavior and departure would change our lives forever? Just sayin'.

CHAPTER FIFTEEN

He doesn't return. Sad to say, it's better this way: No more tempers, no more frightening men, no more erratic, or irrational behavior. Most of all, no more worrying we'll be livin' in a car again. Yet, I wish I felt more at ease. You'd think taking care of Sister, the trailer, school, Mr. Coons, and Butch would keep me occupied and there'd be no time to think about the past. Of all the drama, one scenario haunts me: Watching Mr. Coons with Mama on her deathbed. His display of affection and tenderness plays over and over in my thoughts. One part of me thinks, *let it go*, but the other part pesters *need to know*. Scarlett O'Hara tells me to drop it. I nag.

"Hey, it's our Mama. Don't you think he acted kinda strange? Quite emotional for a stranger?"

"No, forget about it. Who cares?" She can be so callous.

I'm relentless until she gives in, and before she changes her mind, we head over there. Butch comes half way, and we race to the porch where Mr. Coons is cozy in his favorite rocking chair, working a crossword puzzle. I spill it out,

"Mr. Coons, we're sorry to disturb you, but there's something that's been on my mind since Mama died. Sister told me told me to *let it go*, but I've been frettin' and gabbin' about it *for-ever* that it wore her down, and now she agrees we probably need to ask. Sorry if it invades your privacy and all, or hurts your feelings; however, would you explain why you were so tender and emotional when you saw Mama?"

What a relief. But, never in anyone's imagination, overactive or regular, could we have concocted his story.

"I was wondering if you'd get curious enough to ask. I wasn't going to tell you this unless you were ready. I guess I had to be ready too. Well, you have a right to know. Please bear with me. I've carried this with me a long time and need to start at the beginning. I met my wife in a VA hospital while recovering from an Army parachute accident. In a full body cast for months, she was the Red Cross nurse who took care of me. What a beauty with the most exquisite smile and loving nature. We flirted shamelessly, and by the time I got all my parts healed, we were in love. Got married when I could walk down the aisle. Happiest day of my life. Settled here. I was mayor for twelve years and President of the First Bank of Homer for most of my career when I wasn't developing subdivisions. She was a community activist, an artist, and a liaison to the State Office for the Arts and Historical Preservation. The city park was her vision. And, how she loved kids. Wanted a big family. We were ecstatic when our first child—girl—was born—named her Marilyn—after my wife. Then, damn it; an undetected infection set in, and within days of giving birth, my wife died. I was devastated and had no idea how I was going to live—much less raise a child. I had lots of lady friends who offered to help with the secret hope of being the next Mrs. Coons. Yet, I knew then, as I know now, no one would ever replace her. Was determined to raise our daughter like we had planned."

Marilyn? Holy crap. Coincidence, or not? Scarlett O'Hara is messin' with her hair and smackin' her gum. I poke her in her stomach and flash her the "shape it up" look. He proceeds,

"Listen. There's no easy way to tell you," taking in a deep breath, "but I'm your grandfather—your Mama was my daughter." When he stops it's so quiet a funeral would be livelier. We are wide-eyed, open-mouthed, and dumb-founded.

"I know it's a shock, but I hope it'll evidentially make sense. Your mama was an easy child. Never in trouble other than typical growing up shenanigans, like missing curfew, or skipping school, or taking a smoke in the yard. She excelled in school but cared nothing about college or any other school for that matter; however, she loved to draw and paint. What an eye. Exceptional work. Everyone praised her—told her she was destined for great things. But she didn't care. Your grandmother was world-renowned for ceramics. Many museums have her work. Anyway, all hell broke loose when your mama turned eighteen. Told me she'd outgrown Homer. She wanted to move up east. We fought for days. I didn't completely disapprove. Just wanted her to be prepared: have a job, place to live, goals. She'd scoff at my concerns. Called me names; told me I was overbearing and a drag on her life. After one hateful argument, she retreated to her room and didn't come out for a week. When she did, she continued her allegations— told me I failed—totally failed—to understand her needs, and I was denying her the life she desired. I was being selfish! Can you imagine? Selfish. I offered her an apartment in the next town, a new car, anything. She demanded money and a train ticket. If I didn't give in, she'd run away. Such determination; what's a parent to do? Reluctantly, I agreed. Told her once she got settled, I'd open a bank account to help her until she found work. She swore she'd write or call as soon as she arrived in Dunkirk, a town she picked because it had discos, bars, and jobs. When I put her on the train, she flashed me the smile and did the wave, just like Scarlett O'Hara."

His face is flush and you can see the veins in his head and neck, throbbing. When he takes a gulp of water, his trembling hands create waves in the glass. Butch rolls over and groans as if he's having a nightmare; however, it's nothing compared to what we're living this moment. My butt cheeks are numb, but I not moving. This is a serious confession. Sister is mumbling, "No, no, no way. No."

He continues,

"She goes up there; I get one note from her. No phone number or address, nothing, just a card, *I love you*, that's it. I try to find her. Hired a private investigator. It was like she vanished without a trace until a random postcard would give me hope. Always signed, *I love you*. When a card arrived with the clipping of her coronation nothing made sense. New

Albany was in upstate New York and a town no bigger than Homer. But I consoled myself at least she was, somewhere. So, I flew up there. No luck in finding her. Time—hell, years passed and I never heard a word or saw her again until that day." We gasp.

"In my heart—and until I saw her in the trailer—I never felt she was dead; however, I must have been dead to her. It took me a long time to forgive her actions, but I did. I knew I'd grieve forever, but life must go. Doesn't hurt though, to hope for a miracle. And that's what I got. The first time I saw you, I didn't want to believe you might be my grandchildren. Scarlett O'Hara is your Mama's clone for sure. It's hard to deny three generations of Coons' women—you, Lady, have your grandmother's caring, nurturing demeanor and fortitude. You may look like your father, but you're a Coons at heart. How long have I known? Oh, I got suspicious the first time I worked in the trailer. The constantly closed bedroom door and the smoke, bothered me, but it wasn't any of my business. The more time I spent with you, the more it felt like déjà vu. It was cowardly of me not to act on my inklings. Your father was on the go. I was afraid if I took an interest, he'd move you. I couldn't take the chance. Had I known my daughter was lying —suffering—in that bed—I would have found a way to intervene. She's gone—can't change that, but I will do everything I can for you."

His tone is low and his body is collapsed and fatigued. "I'm, embarrassed, ashamed, sad, and most of all so sorry for everything," reaching for his pocket hankie to wipe his hands and face.

Some body knock me in the head and wake me up. Butch's cold, wet nose does the trick. Sister is hiding under a blanket. Mr. Coons slumps in his chair. *Poor man, I hope this roller coaster of emotions doesn't give him a heart attack.* After all, Mama made her choices. Besides, it's not like he could fix our whole life. Then I realize I have one more question.

"Why do you think they picked Homer and the trailer?" A detail I have to know.

His voice is lower and slower than before but determined to finish his story, he puffs up his chest and begins again,

"She grew up in this house. Years ago, the trailer was used when contractors came to town. She must've told your Paw to come and find it. Remember I told you he drove by several times? Guess he needed to be sure it was the right trailer because there's no way she would have known it looked so bad. I figure he probably thought he was looking for something else. Homer hasn't changed too much and lucky for you, she wanted to return. In her condition, I'm shocked she could remember anything. Who knows how she got him to stay, but I bet he never knew the whole story. She could spin a tale if she had to. We'll never know, and it doesn't matter. Whatever she said brought you here. I know she didn't intend to be a bad mother, but she must have been sick a long time. Any illness can rob a person of common sense. She's a Coons—not a monster. More importantly, she knew if you lived here, I'd take care of you."

What an exposé. Out of her hiding place, a snarky Scarlett O'Hara inquires,

"Should we call you some grandfatherly-type name *now*?"

"Not necessarily. It's whatever you want."

Good. Calling him Mr. Coons works. Why change it? Best to keep things as routine as possible. Having a grandfather, wow; who would have thought? Now there's one more person in this insane, melodramatic family. Wonder who else is on our family tree?

Hold it. Before we get Jumpin' Jack goofy, let's think this through. Mr. Coons and the folks kept this secret. Or, at least Mama knew; however, knowing her power over Paw, it probably wasn't too tall of a tale to get him to do this. Why in the world keep good, vital family information a secret? Just proves they had no clue, not one clue, about raisin' kids. How and when did she think we'd find out? Did she think being around her old life would change ours? I seriously doubt it. Let's look at the facts: first, she was too sick to get out of bed, so no chance she'd be involved doin' motherly things; second, Paw was unavailable for any of our needs; third, other than for not stealin' or lyin' we're gypsies or fugitives; and fourth; I'm sure there's a fourth and more, but I can't think. Come to think of it, just who is Paw and what kind of fixin' does he do? A very, very good question. If I ask, I better be ready for the answer I might get. Better to wait. This is a lot to digest for one day. Mr. Coons seems to have aged in front of me, and Scarlett O'Hara, so typical, has resumed rubbing Butch and not offering any emotion, opinion or comment.

It seems, tragically so, I've been betrayed, bamboozled, and lied to my entire life. The hell with anyone else's feelings, this is serious crap. Is this one of those forgiving moments Mr. Coons taught me? Just how does forgiving work when people keep secrets, and they're gone so you can't ask, *why*? Would forgivin' even matter to Paw? Certainly, makes no difference with Mama. I need air.

I walk passed the trailer: It's lit up like a Trekkie spaceship; the shed, now a studio for Scarlett O'Hara, is dark. I head towards it. *Is any of this my fault? For prayin' for a home? For finding the shed, and insisting on the makeover, and meeting Mr. Coons who regained hope about his missing daughter, and revealed a family secret, and will probably have a heart attack because I had questions? And, he had really hard answers. Should I feel guilty? I don't know if a kid my age can have a heart big enough to carry all of this. Who do I pray to now, to help me fix this mess?*

#

A couple hours later I'm standin' in front of the trailer. Scarlett O'Hara is on the step, fuming mad. When she sees me, she waves her arms, and jumps up and down and shrieks,

"How *dare* you leave me? Don't ever, ever, ever, do that again! I thought for sure you were never coming back. Mr. Coons said you'd be back, but damn it, you scared me. Please, don't do that again!" She collapses in my arms like a soggy rag doll.

"I'm sorry. I needed to think. This is toooooooooo much. And I feel so responsible, only I know I shouldn't. All these family problems how and who is gonna help me survive this? We: you, me, Mr. Coons, deserve to be happy, safe. I guess there'll be some serious prayin' tonight. I promise I won't leave you again. And a Fratelli keeps a promise," remembering what Paw told Mama and holding Sister as tight as I can without breaking her.

For the moment, anyway, as for forgiveness, I guess it doesn't matter whether I forgive the folks, or not. We need to move on with a new life—whatever it is. What's done is done. I could be mad as hell at Mr. Coons for keeping all this but there's no way. He did what he thought was right; therefore, sometimes you gotta forgive a little and maybe forget, later.

Besides he's the most level-headed, sane person in this family. Thank goodness I have him 'cause something tells me more complexities of life are right around the corner, and this little secret is only the beginning. Just sayin'.

CHAPTER SIXTEEN

And, so it happens: A major life derailment comes near the end of the school year, Scarlett O'Hara goes off the grid: gets a fake i.d, buys booze and cigarettes, experiments with drugs, shaves her head on one side, straightens and dyes the remaining hair—hot pink, with a skunk stripe down the middle. She's goth in her black leather wardrobe and pasty makeup and robotic movements. When she walks, the heavy chain-link, metal accessories clang and warn me of her approach. She looks like a groupie for Epica. The smell of marijuana saturates her clothes, and she's nocturnal. To get her out of bed to go to the class is a tug of war that's physically and verbally abusive. Her defiance is debilitating. Friends ostracize her, and teachers fear the worst.

"What in the hell are you trying to prove?" I probe one morning, her head obscured by a pillow.

Her clothes, strewn on the floor, reek of booze and smoke, smells I know well. I snatch the pillow from her and fan away the stench.

"You're not my parents or the boss of me—get the hell out of my room."

I hesitate to remind her it's our room. I'll let her be territorial.

"You're absolutely right, but I haven't spent my whole life trying to make things right for you and then you behave like this. You, ungrateful twit. What do you expect to prove with this behavior? You know it won't have a nice ending. This is wrong, totally wrong. What is the matter with *you*?" Anticipating a rational answer from an inconsiderate teenager. Big mistake.

"Wrong with me-you—BITCH?" she screams, throwing a shoe at me. "How *dare* you ask. There's not a damn thing wrong with me that getting out of Homer and away from you won't fix."

"Yeah, rehab in the desert is an idea." I know this sarcasm isn't the best reply.

If looks could kill, I'd be a dead. Her eyes—look at me full of hatred. She points a foil-like fingernail in my direction.

"You *realllly* want to know what's wrong with me? Here it is, Sister. My whole life, you've protected me, coddled me, pushed me. You've been my voice and mind. I have done without question what was expected from you, and anyone else who gave a damn. Why do you think it took me so long to talk? I never had a chance to say anything. And our parents:

Hardly candidates for Parents of the Year! Paw pitching his fits and caring on with Mama like she was some movie star. And, Mama, doped up or drunk all the time—piece of work that woman. Then you—constantly making absurd conversations to keep the tension down." She stops to gather more ugly words, "I had no desire to say anything. Besides, I was going to grow up to be a beauty queen, remember? Beauty and brains, crap. What a friggin' curse. This trailer is a piece of crap; I want all the money from my sketches! Why can't we live in a real house? I hate you. Besides, how totally ignorant of you not to know our father was a mobster—a hired gun, a felonious criminal. If I stray and screw up, it's in my DNA. On both sides. I want out-o-u-t. The sooner the better."

I fire back,

"Hold on a damn minute. You hate me. Fine! Blame me for all your screw-ups; go for it. I'm sorry—not that you give a rat's ass about apologies. Just where in the world do you come off calling Paw *mobster*?"

My composure escapes me, and I want to shake her. What a mean-spirited brat.

"Have you ever looked in the P-R-A-D-A or one of those suitcases? You go in that hell hole of a bedroom and look; right now. There's all the proof you need."

I admit, generally inquisitive, I wasn't interested in snooping. Besides, being in their room was repulsive.

"I don't believe you."

"That is *soooo* like you. Such a Pollyanna. Some people are evil, wicked, evil. Go see for yourself, damn it. I'm not lying. I'll show you."

First time she's been helpful. Could be progress. I don't know what upsets me more: she violated their privacy, or the fact she knows things I don't and has kept her discoveries to herself. More secrets.

The room is haunted. I feel their presence; I swear I hear their favorite music and see their entwined profile on the walls. The impression in the middle of the bed has become home to bugs and the entire room is shrouded in stagnant smoke. I'm ashamed of its condition. The wedding picture is missing. It's stifling in the airless room. Sister drags the suitcases and the P-R-A-D-A to the kitchen.

"See for yourself."

The P-R-A-D-A is threadbare, and the handle is broken in half. Inside is a gun in a shoulder holster.

"It's a Glock," she informs me. There's a smaller gun and boxes of bullets. This one makes a great concealed weapon," she adds, sounding like an expert from the NRA.

Digging deeper, we find an assortment of illegal equipment: miniature smoke bombs, brass knuckles, canisters of pepper spray, tools for picking locks, and two, inactive cell phones all squashed on the bottom. Pairs of handcuffs and a wool hood fill up the rest of the purse. And, there's a grenade. I feel like I'm looking at evidence from crime shows. These still don't prove he's a hoodlum.

Next, she splits apart the case with the making-up kit. She deposits the contents on the couch. Mama's ragged clothes fall to the ground. There's a concealed compartment under all the garments. She unzips it to reveal a stack of disintegrating newspaper clippings:

Dateline, Chicago: *Pete Fratelli, Pete the Rat, reputed boss of the Fratelli family, is sought in connection with the assassination of rival Louie the Louse Morelli. Morelli's beaten and bound body was found when Chicago construction workers imploded a building. Fratelli's signature shot, a single bullet to the heart was cause of death.*

Dateline Las Vegas: *Last night, the Flamingo Casino was robbed by a gang from the Fratelli family of New York. The gang, led by Pete Fratelli, reportedly stole millions. Witnesses say the thugs were well dressed and did nothing to hide their identities. A $ 100,000 reward has been posted for information leading to their arrest.*

Dateline Washington, D.C.: *Today, authorities announced the addition of long-time mobster, Pete Fratelli, to the FBI's Ten Most Wanted List. Fratelli's last hit was the murder of several "debtors" in Chinatown. Each one shot once through the heart. The carnage filled the walk-in freezer at Chin's Dumpling House.*

Gruesome photographs. There are several FBI flyers with his unflattering mug shot. He's their number one felon. This can't be. What a hypocrite! A thief, a liar, a *killer*. That man, how *could* he?? This is what a fixer does? He's a hired gun? In the *mob*? He helps gangsters? Has to be a mistake. The troublemaker must be an identical twin. I look at Scarlett O'Hara who's standing with hands on her hips and looking quite pleased with herself.

"See?" she says in a high and mighty tone of voice.

"How long have you known?"

"Not long. You were at school, and I was home with a hangover, only I told you it was the flu. Ever since Mr. Coons told his story, I wondered if there was more. Wanted to see if Mama saved something, anything about our family. Don't know why I cared, but I did. I went digging through their things. In a pocket in the P-R-A-D-A I found our crumbled birth certificates. I knew it! There had to be more. When I read the articles, it made sense: the years on the road, small towns, his short and long-term absences, the jail break—they recognized him—and it wasn't going to end well—that was always his fear. No way he was going to jail. I'd like to think he ran to save his family, but with all these secrets, who knows? Then his disposition—fight or flight; and our lifestyle—some months we had money, others not. A family on the lam. A mobster's family. Our own gangster movie. I'm surprised Mama didn't name you or me Bonnie Parker."

This information puts a cannonball size hole in my gut which surprises me because ever since Mr. Coons' revelation, almost nothing gets me worked up. Now, even though I hear her words I don't comprehend the magnitude of Paw's career until I realize holy crap—Mama. She was his willing accomplice! How could she love him *that* much? What was she *thinking* hooking up with a mobster? And kids! Accidents. Two accidents. Now I'm certain we were never part of their plan. She was probably relieved when they told her no more babies. I can only hope the answers are in the locket or her making-up kit because our family story is becoming more and more like a really bad movie. I suck up the pain and return to the task of finding the locket. Scarlett O'Hara has retreated to couch and shows no interest in my search.

In the kit, the cosmetics are dried out; the lipstick is smushed; the brushes are without many of its bristles, the jewels, and her possessions are all neatly wrapped in satin pouches. I don't see the locket. My gut starts gurgling. I ramp up my search. It's nowhere.

"Hey, have you ever touched any of this without me?"

I'm gonna be really peeved if Scarlett O'Hara's borrowed without telling.

"Hell no! and, why would I? You're such a control freak—you'd probably have me arrested."

"Hey, cut the crap. You're right, 100% right. I'm sorry—again. The locket, do you remember it? I have to find it."

"Sorry, I don't remember any locket. Maybe you imagined it? I have no idea. Besides, this is all junk."

"How dare you say this is junk? I mean, I'm no jeweler but this has to be worth something. We need to keep looking. You started this, so now we have to finish. We're going to find something special; I know it. Come on, help me."

"Should we try the other suitcase?" she asks.

Good idea. The weight of the case is deceiving and it requires all our strength to move it. The rusty clasp won't budge without a saw or a cutter. Determined and angry at this deterrence, I start kicking and beating it.

"Hold on a second," Sister shouts in horror as I mutilate the case. "You're acting like–like–a maniac. You're frightening me! What's happening?"

My frenzy continues. I'm out of control. My body is on fire, and my gut is about to erupt. She screams louder. Not at me, but at the most horrible, nasty, vulgar, ugly, no doubt, mean-ass-Hulk-looking human being barreling through the front door. He backhands her—w*hack*—and she hits the floor. Blood puddles around her head. She doesn't whimper. In spite of his obesity and tree stump legs, he lunges at me but I don't move. I figure if he's killed Sister, he can kill me, too—I don't want to live without her. *Shoot me*, I think. When he's almost on top of me, I recognize him. HIM! One of the goons from the ebony-colored car.

"Where's the money?" he chortles, waving a huge gun at me. "Don't go playing dumb broad with me. You've got it; I know it so give it up."

Money? Here?

"Your Paw took it, and I want it. He wouldn't tell me either—so I killed him. You're next."

"MURDERER!" I screech.

"That's right, shaweeeet-hart," hissing through his clinched teeth. "He was a worthless, stupid man. And your Mama was a whore. What a pair."

He knew Mama too? If I live long enough, he might tell me more. Who am I kiddin'? I'm a goner.

"I don't know anything about money."

I feel the rush of adrenaline and the Fratelli confidence, but nose to nose, his sewer breath and toxic spit makes me nauseous, and I start to gag. He presses the nozzle of the gun on my forehead. I don't dare cry or fight—not yet—I know I have one chance to make a break—the strategy has to be perfect. Thank goodness thinking on my feet is my specialty.

"I ain't got all day. Give it to me, or we're gonna have some fun . . . and then I'll kill you."

Fun? I doubt we share the same idea of fun. I'm getting cross-eyed from looking at the gun. I can hardly stand all his odors, but as long as we keep talkin', he's not killin'.

"Let's think about this. If the money were here, and I'm still saying it isn't—where do think it would be? In this suitcase? Or this one? How about in the freezer? Or under the floor? Maybe under the mattress? I bet that's where it is. Why don't you look?" All viable suggestions if you ask me.

If I can get him moving, I can find a way to disarm him and escape. Instead, he pistols whips me but not enough to knock me out. I can hear him rummaging through the trailer. No sound from Sister. When I start to moan, he hits me, harder and harder, until I lose consciousness. Strange memories drift in and out of my brutalized head:

> *Middle of the night. Mama walking out of the trailer all dressed up in a slinky silver lamé dress, sky-high metallic stilettos, her hair, magnificently coiffed, framing her face and tumbling down her back. Stumbling in her too high heels— or her drunken state—she tries to walk like a model. She gets in a car only to return hours later looking like a spectacle: lipstick smeared over her face, mascara-streaked cheeks, blood dripping from her nose; her outfit—torn and hanging off her shoulders. No shoes. I rush to help. She pushes me away and gimps to her room.*

> *We're at Lake Mead. The folks are smooching and cooing under a striped umbrella. I'm up to my knees in the crystal turquoise water. Paw buys corn dogs, fries, and ice-cold Coke floats from a food truck. Scarlett O'Hara makes clown faces with mustard splotches on our cheeks and catsup noses. The folks take pictures.*

> *New bikes from Mr. Coons for no particular occasion. Mine gold, hers sapphire—him holding on until we get our balance. Butch running behind. Rolling in the grass—laughing. Butch licking our faces.*

> *Our first church service. Dressed in new clothes. Heavenly choir and organ music loud enough for angels to hear. We're reciting the prayers. Afterwards we go to brunch with Mr. Coons and swim in the pool he's built in his yard.*

I hear, chanting . . .

#

It's dark when I regain consciousness, but completely disoriented and hyperventilating. Excruciating pain rips through me when I try to move. I have to escape; I'm not dying here. Scarlett O'Hara, oh my god, what's happened to her? Slithering like a snake, inch by inch through the blood, I struggle to find her.

"*Scarlett O'Hara, where are you?*" I cry, only nothing comes out of my swollen mouth. *Think, Lady. What would Paw tell you to do? Probably, "Quit whining and get the hell out of there. And, don't look back."* Can't do that just yet. I'm not abandoning her—alive or dead. On my belly, clawing the dried blood out of my nearly useless eyes, I see her—a gun in one hand and the locket in the other—standing over the hoodlum's lifeless body. The gun aimed at his heart.

"Oh . . . Scarlett O'Hara . . . ." Passing out before I can finish.

#

Don't know how the EMS, police, and Mr. Coons knew to come to our rescue but when the posse arrives, my body looks like a question mark. Hallucinating, I see two Scarlett O'Haras. I reach out to touch one of them. Both disappear. Muffled voices, strong hands, and flashes of light play havoc in my head. In the hospital, my clothes are cut off and I'm probed, poked, and manipulated under bright lights and pushed through ear-splitting cylindrical machines. I panic and thrash when I don't see her. They sedate me—probably for days.

The interrogations are endless: poker-faced police nod and humph, and in unison say their condescending and suspicious, "That so." To make it more sinister there's no gun at the crime scene which befuddles them; however, whether together or alone, our story is the same: home invasion, self-defense. We have no idea what happened to the gun. I don't care if I ever see it again. Miraculously there's never a mention of the incident in the *Homer Gazette*.

Two months later, recovering at Mr. Coons' house, Scarlett O'Hara peers over a crime novel she's reading and asks,

"Think there's any money?"

"Are you nuts? After all we've been through, you're thinking about the money? You need another brain scan."

"How about a treasure hunt? Aren't you a little bit curious?"

"No and HELL no!"

"Such a party-pooper! I'm *sooooo* disappointed. Come on. It'll be fun. If I find it myself, I might not share," she says, acting all cocky.

What did the doctors do with my Scarlett O'Hara? Did she have an out-of-body experiences and is possessed? Morphine-that's it. The narcotic in the hospital stole the rational part of her. Go on a treasure hunt? Seriously?

"Come on, come on. I'd do it if you asked. Please? You were always such a thrill-seeker. Come *onnnnnnn*." I wish she'd go back to being speechless. No luck. "One time—in my whole life—I ask for an adventure, and you get hardheaded. Honestly. What's your problem? Afraid of what we might find?"

"I'm not afraid of nothin'. Ok, damn it. What are you proposin'?

"Go back to the trailer."

Now, I'm positive they gave her electric shock treatments and messed up her brain. The structure is boarded up with an around the clock security guard. He'll sideline this preposterous idea.

"Are you sure you want to do this? Say we get passed the gestapo—then what? We have no idea the suitcase is still there."

"Do I have to *explain* everything?"

I knew it—she has no idea; however, as I think about it, returning to the scene might be a start. Works in the movies.

She charms the guard into taking a long break. Tells him we have to gather up her art, and it will take a long time. Reassures him he won't get fired if Mr. Coons finds out he left his post. She murmurs it's super important not to tell anyone. Flashes him the grin. He can't scoot away fast enough. What a con. And why does this performance surprise me? Guess I still want to be a little naïve about my family and their peculiarities.

The spots where the thug bled out and her blood have been bleached. A chalk outline of my body is barely visible. She's wandering around. I'm waiting for her to tell me what to do. Out of their bedroom, she calls,

"Lady, I need you," sounding strangely like Mama.

Smoke seeps from the room, but there's no lit cigarette: there's music—but no radio and their voices—are hushed and seductive. Scarlett O'Hara is perched on top of the suitcase wearing Mama's dilapidated crown.

"You ready for the hunt?"

As ready as I'll ever be. Just sayin'.

CHAPTER SEVENTEEN

The clasp falls, and we open the case. The smell is repugnant and Scarlett O'Hara slams the lid.

"Can't stand a little stink?"

"O…shut…up," she hisses back. Opens it again. Holding our noses, we begin exploring.

There's a scrapbook: photos of our young mother wearing a high school cheerleader uniform and saddle shoes, holding pom-poms while balanced on the shoulders of a jock in a varsity jacket and crew cut; prom night, radiant in a voluminous gown standing two inches taller than her date; and a class picture surrounded by her friends. Her Homer High

School Yearbook is full of autographs, each salutation praising her talents, friendships or offering good luck wishes:

> *Dear Marilyn, You're my best friend. I will miss you; let's never lose touch, Love, Mandy.*

> *Marilyn, senior year has been a blast. Good luck with your art. Come see me at State. Love, Jake.*

> *Marilyn, follow your passion and your dreams; you will be successful in life and love, Regards, Miss Kelly.*

> *Congratulations on winning Outstanding Senior; you earned it, Mel.*

Preserved between layers of tissue is pair of scuffed pink pointe shoes and a sparkly tulle tutu. An evening bag is full of frilly hair bows and sequined barrettes. In a box is a sterling heart charm on a small bangle bracelet, engraved, *Happy Graduation, Love Dad.*

We're in awe of this priceless memorabilia and meticulously continue perusing it. Her heavy art books flatten posters and playbills. A diminutive prayer book, the size of a pack of cigarettes, is ironically wedged between two full cartons. Metal military dog tags, a nurse's cap, and a Red Cross pin are tucked in a baby blanket.

A shocker: Stacks of letters without addresses or stamps labeled, 'To Pete' are tied together with grosgrain ribbons. Secured with rubber bands is an assortment of holiday and sentimental Hallmark greeting cards: anniversary, birthday, and Valentine's Day—all for Mama—and signed, *I love you, Pete.*

There's a note,

My darling Pete,

I dread the day you leave and count my heart beats until you return. I will die soon—I know it. You are my spirit, my love. Without you, there is no sunset or sunrise. I am yours unconditionally in life and forever in death.

All my love and being, Marilyn

Another,

Pete,

I will follow you anywhere. I will never doubt you or ask questions. I am yours—you have my trust and fidelity. I will walk with you in danger and joy.

All my love and being, Marilyn

In an envelope is a creased black and white photo of a beaming couple on the deck of a ship. The caption reads, 'Giovanni and Rose Fratelli, Ellis Island, 1912.' Stapled to it is a photo of two youngsters in front of a church, 'Frank and Pete, Easter,' but no date. A rosary with the cross missing and two plain gold wedding rings are in a disintegrating hankie. Another envelope is addressed to Sister and me. She rips it open,

To our daughters,

We apologize for the pain and hurt we have caused. We know you have suffered. But we do not apologize for our lifestyle and the years on the road. It was the best way to take care of you. We love you and are devoted to you as we have been to each other. Where would you have learned to dance on a whim? or sleep under the stars? or think on your feet to avoid danger? The adventures and endless journeys were to teach you how to survive life, to help you develop resilience but most of all to show you the power of unconditional love. We want you to aspire to a better and grander life, but unless one experiences the struggles, triumphs mean little. You both have talents and potential to set the world on fire—in a good way!

Paw is not proud of his career and we're not proud of some of our actions, but we will forever be proud of both of you. Death ends a life but not a relationship. Please forgive and love us in death as we loved you in life.

Mama and Paw

"Hal-le-lu-jah! . . . Praise the Lord! . . . Amen! . . . Hal-le-lu-jah!"

I'm acting like I'm at a church revival: bowing and crossing, and doing a jig like I'm dancing across hot coals. Tears. Lots of happy tears.

"I don't understand," Sister says shaking out the letter.

"You don't? You're kiddin' me, right? Are you serious?"

"No. You better explain it to me 'cause I'm not feeling whatever it is you're feeling." she says indifferently.

"Oh, Scarlett O'Hara, it's our happy ending! THEY LOVED US! We're their greatest achievement! Accomplished through love. Can't get any better than that! Sure, life could have been better, easier, and certainly happier, but they did their best. Besides, they had plenty of reasons to be isolated. How long have we wondered why? Growing up feeling they only loved each other, although Mama did say, 'I love you,' once. Paw, he was a complicated man. He insisted we learn the right life lessons while he was runnin' and killin' and tryin' to take care of a wife, and two girls who needed more than he could provide. He was noble, sort of, but most of all, they wanted their daughters to thrive, not just survive. Sure, their methods were unorthodox. They had to do it their way. Now, we're liberated from a lifetime of wondering why not the billboard house and movie life. Like it or not, deliberate or not, this is exactly the life they intended. And, the best part—they kept their promise—everything is all right."

"So, you think everything is all right?" She says still sounding apprehensive.

"Hell, yeah. I mean, it's not cool our father was a hired gun or we lived the way we did—I mean—they never wanted to draw attention to their children, or themselves. We almost got killed because of money we may not have. Just imagine if we lived in a billboard house, spent a lot of money, and people asked questions? I doubt we could have survived. We had to stay way under the radar. But I think that's what made them love even more. The constant threat something might happen. Would it have made a difference if we grew up knowing all this? Maybe. At least we, or I, would have felt our lifestyle was justified. But knowin' Paw was a killer has been the worst. Yet in some demented way it boils down to love. Who would have thought? This makes a killer love story. Come on, let's get outta here and go tell Mr. Coons." I begin to skip out of the room.

"You can't go yet. We haven't found the money! It's got to be here; I know it," she yells.

Damn, the money. Do we really want to find it? Paw died because of it. Mama died because she wanted me to be free of taking care of her so we'd have a real life with Mr. Coons. Finding money now might change our lives in ways we—who knows? Finding it, having it, possibly using it, are we really ready for such a drastic lifestyle change? Guess we won't know unless we look for it.

Hell-bent on finding it out—or not—none of what I've said seems to matter to her. She begins recklessly ripping through the case, pulling up the cardboard bottom. And damn, there it is . . . the money: wads of ones, tens, twenties, and hundreds, and hundreds of hundred-dollar bills. No telling how much the stash is worth. Just when I thought it all made sense.

We start throwing it around the room, blanketing the floor like confetti. Wait. *What the hell? What malarkey is this?* Everything I was feeling about love and the right thing, shattered. We lived in poverty—while they slept with a fortune? I mean why couldn't they, spend a little to make life a bit more, livable? *Come on.* I'm not feeling, loved, forgiving or free. This is too much. The smirk on Scarlett O'Hara's face tells me she's quite proud of herself, and I expect an, "I told you so." I'm in no mood for self-righteousness. A note drops out from one of the stacks:

> *This is hush money—money that kept you safe and Paw out of jail. Some may try to steal it from you, but it's yours. Don't worry about the jewels. We considered them 'investments,' so share them equally. Now you must go to the locket. It will explain everything. Please don't be angry.*
>
> *Paw and Mama.*

They are something else. Have an explanation for everything. If they were so damn clever why all this mystery movie crap? I'm not sure I can take more of their posthumous scavenger hunts. Scarlett O'Hara is lying in the money. I can only hope the locket will be the last of this charade.

"Hey, *where* is the locket?" Trying to hold down the frustration in my voice and not take it out on her.

"You mean this?" She asks slyly as she removes it from another compartment, rather than hand it to me, drops it in front of me.

"Between killers and money and all these friggin' secrets, do you have any idea how upset I am? Cut the attitude. Right now, I want to say the hell with all of this and you, but I'm not giving up. You may not remember, or care, but Mama believed the locket had some strange power. In spite of her inability to be sober and a decent mother, I need to find out for myself if I imagined magic, or whether I'm just as messed up as everyone else in this family."

My tirade doesn't faze her one bit. She's still mesmerized by the cash, juggling the bundles and spreading them all over the floor. Up until today, I didn't think to ask how or why she had the locket during the home invasion or where it's been since. Finally, holding it—more tarnished—my suspicions about to be reconciled—whatever happens Mama and Paw deemed it. Maybe it's because of a little hocus-pocus we've survived?

"For your information—I always felt there was something special about this locket, but never shared my thoughts with you or anyone else. Before I open this, did you ever notice any kind of phenomenon when Mama stroked it during Paw's tantrums or when we were in sticky situations? Like the jailbreak, or when we had to fight the crook?"

"*Noooo*," she says, with dramatic flair. "Was I holding a locket?"

Her face goes ashen like Mama's—her eyes watching . . . nothing. There's no response when I BOO her. She's picked a fine time to go up in her head. I start to open the locket, but the tiny hinge is as tight as a clam. I shake it. Try again. Nothing happens. Without looking at me, she reaches over and takes it out of my hand. Her nimble fingers separate it.

Two strips of paper—no bigger than a Chinese fortune—pop out from each side. Like a closed accordion, they are pleated so tightly it's difficult to open them. She carefully stretches one and gives it to me to read:

Force and power are not the way to love

She rocks back and forth. I toy with the other piece, overcome with trepidation and dread. I don't want to read it. An invisible glue-like substance covers my hand and the miniscule piece sticks to them. I gently try to pull it off, but the piece remains. Is this a cruel trick or what?

"What's the matter? Magic got you stumped?" Mocking me.

"So, you do believe it has special powers?" Thinking what a break-through. We agree.

"Hell no! I found the money. The rest is such crap."

What a Debbie-downer. Just when I thought, but oh, well, hell, I don't care what she thinks.

"Fine. I'll figure it out. Like always—if I want anything done, I have to do it myself. You are just like her. Sit and pout. Spoiled. Insensitive. You wait and see."

Without warning, the other paper springs open. On it,

Believe and forgive

Simple as that. Their last lesson. No magic. Fine. Does this mean it's time to be regular people just because they left behind words of wisdom and money? I mean, we *aren't* about to live by example! This is no Hollywood movie. They paid for our freedom, but are we really *free*? Yet . . .I do feel liberated from something that has had me in a vice, crushing me, robbing me of every minute of my youth. Time to believe . . . Lady, YOU ARE FREE! Forgive? That's all I've done. Don't know how's that's gonna work now. Why don't I feel more victorious? This is a costly, tragic, victory. A Pyrrhic victory. And is the prize worth all this pain? I look over at Scarlett O'Hara who is regaining color and has a huge, wicked, grin.

"Lady, I'm truly sorry. For everything. I get it now. All of it. But I doubt we're hardly free—at least not yet."

Without warning and before I can stop her, she takes handfuls of money and throws it out in to the moonless sky. The wind catches it and blows it out of reach. A magnetic force seals me to the floor. All I can do is watch—stunned—our money, going, going, gone.

"*What are you doing? Have you gone mad?*" I yell, but she doesn't stop.

When she goes to the door for the umpteenth time, it slams shuts and locks before she can continue her maliciousness. Without warning we are overcome with the profuse smell of mint and lilacs and thunderous music. "S . . .T!" screams Sister, but I can barely hear her. I try to move again. Stuck. Realizing I'm immobile, her panic increases, and she runs full speed towards me, fists flying. I squeeze the locket, and abruptly her movements become labored and controlled. With each step she takes, my body is getting lighter and I feel my feet. By the time she reaches me, I'm loose and she collides in to me like a bowling ball hitting a pin. Fatigued we sit, comforted by the quiet, still, scentless air of the room decorated with money—everywhere. This is it. We. Are. Free. Just sayin."

KUDOS

To my family. Without your love and support my world would only be black and white instead of the plethora of color I see every day, and thank you, for the wealth of memories, experiences, and adventures we share. And most of all— to Nicholas and Luke; my forever adorables.

To the talent and support behind this debut:

Marian Rosse, for her sharp editing, Janet Meyer, who told me to, "think big," Cindy Schumacher for literary insight, and Pat Sekaris for spending time with Lady.

Carol McDavid and Troy Harrison, my techno gurus.

Pam Veto and T.O…Just sayin'

To the published authors I reached out to for advice and direction, especially Carolyn Breckinridge and Greg Triggs.

And to Mitch . . .for years of unconditional support and love.

About the Author

K at Tauber is an experienced writer, an international corporate special event producer, public speaker, clinical nutritionist, and culinary instructor.

Her work has appeared on her blog, *Move Over Stephanie Klein*, and in numerous trade publications. A debut novel, she was inspired when an elderly aunt commented, "You never really know your relatives." After completing a NaNoWriMo challenge, *Secrets*, was born.

A native of Chicago, Illinois, she received her B.A. in English and History from Texas Christian University, and her M.L.A. from Houston Baptist University. She currently resides in Houston, Texas, without cats or dogs. When not writing, Kat enjoys reading, cooking, and walking on the beach. Visit her website at www.kattauber19.com or contact her at kattauber19@gmail.com.

Secrets: powerful, magical, and a killer.

-KGT

Write your Secrets here.